East Side Manor

East Side Manor

THE OVERLOOK

ALSO BY MICHAEL CONNELLY

Fiction

The Black Echo

The Black Ice

The Concrete Blonde

The Last Coyote

The Poet

Trunk Music

Blood Work

Angels Flight

Void Moon

A Darkness More Than Night

City of Bones

Chasing the Dime

Lost Light

The Narrows

The Closers

The Lincoln Lawyer

Echo Park

Nonfiction

Crime Beat

THE OVERLOOK

A NOVEL BY

MICHAEL CONNELLY

**Doubleday Large Print
Home Library Edition**

LITTLE, BROWN AND COMPANY
NEW YORK BOSTON LONDON

Little, Brown and Company
Hachette Book Group USA
237 Park Avenue, New York, NY 10169

Portions of this novel were originally published in se-rial form in the *New York Times Magazine*.

The characters and events in this book are fictitious. Any similarity to real persons, living or dead, is coinci-dental and not intended by the author.

ISBN 978-0-7394-8118-9

Printed in the United States of America

**This Large Print Book carries the
Seal of Approval of N.A.V.H.**

To the librarian who gave me
To Kill a Mockingbird

THE
OVERLOOK

ONE

THE CALL CAME AT MIDNIGHT. Harry Bosch was awake and sitting in the living room in the dark. He liked to think that he was doing this because it allowed him to hear the saxophone better. By masking one of the senses he accentuated another.

But deep down he knew the truth. He was waiting.

The call was from Larry Gandle, his supervisor in Homicide Special. It was Bosch's first call out in the new job. And it was what he had been waiting for.

"Harry, you up?"

"I'm up."

"Who's that you got playing?"

"Frank Morgan, live at the Jazz Standard in New York. That's George Cables you're hearing now on piano."

"Sounds like 'All Blues.'"

"You nailed it."

"Good stuff. I hate to take you away from it."

Bosch used the remote to turn the music off.

"What's the call, Lieutenant?"

"Hollywood wants you and Iggy to come out and take over a case. They've already caught three today and can't handle a fourth. This one also looks like it might become a hobby. It looks like an execution."

The Los Angeles Police Department had seventeen geographic divisions, each with its own station and detective bureau, including a homicide squad. But the divisional squads were the first line and couldn't get bogged down on long-running cases. When a murder came with any sort of political, celebrity or media attachment, it was usually shuttled down to Homicide Special, which operated out of the Robbery-Homicide Division in Parker Center. Any case that appeared to be particularly difficult and time-consuming—that would invariably stay active like a hobby—would also be an immediate candidate for Homicide Special. This was one of those.

"Where is it?" Bosch asked.

"Up on that overlook above the Mulholland Dam. You know the place?"

"Yeah, I've been up there."

Bosch got up and walked to the dining room table. He opened a drawer designed for silverware and took out a pen and a small notebook. On the first page of the notebook he wrote down the date and the location of the murder scene.

"Any other details I should know?" Bosch asked.

"Not a lot," Gandle said. "Like I said, it was described to me as an execution. Two in the back of the head. Somebody took this guy up there and blew his brains out all over that pretty view."

Bosch let this register a moment before asking the next question.

"Do they know who the dead guy is?"

"The divisionals are working on it. Maybe they'll have something by the time you get over there. It's practically in your neighborhood, right?"

"Not too far."

Gandle gave Bosch more specifics on the location of the crime scene and asked if Harry would make the next call out to his partner. Bosch said he would take care of it.

"Okay, Harry, get up there and see what's what, then call me and let me know. Just wake me up. Everybody else does."

Bosch thought it was just like a supervisor to complain about getting woken up to a person he would routinely wake up over the course of their relationship.

"You got it," Bosch said.

Bosch hung up and immediately called Ignacio Ferras, his new partner. They were still feeling their way. Ferras was more than twenty years younger and from another culture. The bonding would happen, Bosch was sure, but it would come slowly. It always did.

Ferras was awakened by Bosch's call but became alert quickly and seemed eager to respond, which was good. The only problem was that he lived all the way out in Diamond Bar, which would put his ETA at the crime scene at least an hour off. Bosch had talked to him about it the first day they had been assigned as partners but Ferras wasn't interested in moving. He had a family support system in Diamond Bar and wanted to keep it.

Bosch knew that he would get to the crime scene well ahead of Ferras and that would mean he would have to handle any divisional friction on his own. Taking a case away from the divisional squad was always a delicate thing. It was a decision usually made by supervisors, not by the homicide detectives on the scene. No homicide detective worth the gold trim on his badge would ever want to give away a case. That just wasn't part of the mission.

"See you there, Ignacio," Bosch said.

"Harry," Ferras said, "I told you. Call me Iggy. Everybody does."

Bosch said nothing. He didn't want to call him Iggy. He didn't think it was a name that matched the weight of the assignment and mission. He wished that his partner would come to that realization and then stop asking him.

Bosch thought of something and added an instruction, telling Ferras to swing by Parker Center on his way in and pick up the city car they were assigned. It would add minutes to his arrival time but Bosch planned to drive his own car to the scene and he knew he was low on gas.

"Okay, see you there," Bosch said, leaving names out.

He hung up and grabbed his coat out of the closet by the front door. As he put his arms into it he glanced at himself in the mirror on the inside of the door. At fifty-six years old he was trim and fit and could even stand to add a few pounds, while other detectives his age were getting round in the middle. In Homicide Special, there was a pair of detectives known as Crate and Barrel because of their widening dimensions. Bosch didn't have to worry about that.

The gray had not yet chased all of the brown out of his hair but it was getting close to victory. His dark eyes were clear and bright and ready for the challenge awaiting him at the overlook. In his own eyes Bosch saw a basic understanding of homicide work, that when he stepped out the front door he would be willing and able to go the distance—whatever that entailed—to get the job done. It made him feel as though he were bulletproof.

He reached across his body with his left hand to pull the gun out of the holster on his right hip. It was a Kimber Ultra Carry. He quickly checked the magazine and the action and then returned the weapon to its holster.

He was ready. He opened the door.

The lieutenant had not known a lot about the case but he had been right about one thing. The crime scene was not far from Bosch's home. He dropped down to Cahuenga and then took Barham across the 101 Freeway. From there it was a quick run up Lake Hollywood Drive to a neighborhood of homes clustered on the hills surrounding the reservoir and the Mulholland Dam. They were expensive homes.

He worked his way around the fenced reservoir, stopping only for a moment when he came upon a coyote in the road. The animal's eyes caught the headlights and glowed brightly. It then turned and sauntered slowly across the road, disappearing into the brush. It was in no hurry to get out of the way, almost daring Bosch to do something. It reminded him of his days on patrol, when he saw the same challenge in the eyes of most of the young men he encountered on the street.

After passing the reservoir he took Tahoe Drive farther up into the hills and then connected with the eastern terminus of Mulholland Drive. There was an unofficial overlook of the city here. It was posted with NO PARKING and OVERLOOK CLOSED AT DARK signs. But these were routinely ignored at all hours of the day and night.

Bosch pulled in behind the grouping of official vehicles—the Forensics van and the coroner's wagon as well as several marked and unmarked police cars. There was an outer perimeter of yellow police tape surrounding the crime scene and inside this boundary was a silver Porsche Carrera with its hood open. It had been sectioned off by more yellow tape and this told Bosch that it was most likely the victim's car.

Bosch parked and got out. A patrol officer assigned to the outer perimeter took down his name and badge number—2997—and allowed him under the yellow tape. He approached the crime scene. Two banks of portable lights had been erected on either side of the body, which was in the center of a clearing that looked down upon the city. As Bosch approached he saw forensics techs and coroner's people working on and around the body. A tech with a video camera was documenting the scene as well.

"Harry, over here."

Bosch turned and saw Detective Jerry Edgar leaning against the hood of an unmarked detective cruiser. He had a cup of coffee in his hand and appeared to be just waiting. He pushed himself off the car as Bosch came over.

Edgar had been Bosch's partner once, back when he had worked in Hollywood Division. Back then Bosch was a team leader on the homicide squad. Now Edgar was in that position.

"Been waiting on somebody from RHD," Edgar said. "Didn't know it would be you, man."

"It's me."

"You working this solo?"

"No, my partner's on the way."

"Your new partner, right? I haven't heard from you since that mess over in Echo Park last year."

"Yeah. So what do you have here?"

Bosch didn't want to talk about Echo Park with Edgar. With anyone, as a matter of fact. He wanted to stay focused on the case at hand. It was his first call out since his transfer to Homicide Special. He knew there would be a lot of people watching his moves. Some of them would be people hoping he would fail.

Edgar turned so that Bosch could see what was spread out on the trunk of the car. Bosch took out glasses and put them on as he leaned in close to look. There wasn't a lot of light but he could see an array of evidence bags. The bags separately contained items taken from the body. These included a wallet, a key ring and a clip-on name tag. There was also a money clip with a thick fold of currency and a BlackBerry that was still on, its green light flashing and ready to transmit calls its owner would never make or receive.

"The coroner's guy just gave me all of this," Edgar said. "They should be done with the body in about ten minutes."

Bosch picked up the bag containing the ID tag and angled it toward the light. It said Saint Agatha's Clinic for Women. On it was a photograph of a man with dark hair and dark eyes. It identified him as Dr. Stanley Kent. He was smiling at the camera. Bosch noticed that the ID tag was also a swipe key that could open locked doors.

"You talk to Kiz much?" Edgar asked.

It was a reference to Bosch's former partner, who had transferred after Echo Park to a management job in the OCP—the office of the chief of police.

"Not too much. But she's doing fine."

Bosch moved on to the other evidence bags and wanted to move the conversation away from Kiz Rider and onto the case at hand.

"Why don't you run down what you've got for me, Jerry?" he said.

"Happy to," Edgar said. "The stiff was found about an hour ago. As you can see from the signs out on the street, there is no parking up here and no loitering after dark. Hollywood always has a patrol swing by here a few times a night to chase lookyloos away. Keeps the rich locals up here happy. I am told that house over there is Madonna's. Or it was."

He pointed to a sprawling mansion about a hundred yards from the clearing. The moonlight silhouetted a tower rising from the structure. The mansion's exterior was striped in alternating hues of rust and yellow like a Tuscan church. It was on a promontory that afforded anyone looking through its windows a magnificent, sweeping view of the city below. Bosch imagined the pop star up in the tower looking down on the city that lay at her command.

Bosch looked back at his old partner, ready for the rest of the report.

"The patrol car swings around about eleven and sees the Porsche with the hood open. Engine's in the back of those Porsches, Harry. It means the trunk was open."

"Got it."

"Okay, so you knew that already. Anyway, the patrol car pulls up, they don't see anybody in or around the Porsche, so the two officers get out. One of them walks out into the clearing and finds our guy. He's facedown and has two in the back of the head. An execution, clean and simple."

Bosch nodded at the ID tag in the evidence bag.

"And this is the guy, Stanley Kent?"

"Looks that way. The tag and the wallet both say he's Stanley Kent, forty-two years old from just around the corner on Arrowhead Drive. We ran the plate on the Porsche and it comes back to a business called K and K Medical Physicists. I just ran Kent through the box and he came up pretty clean. He's got a few speeding tickets on the Porsche but that's it. A straight shooter."

Bosch nodded as he registered all the information.

"You are going to get no grief from me, taking over this case, Harry," Edgar said. "I got one partner in court this month and I left my other one at the first scene we caught to-day—a three-bagger with a fourth victim on life support at Queen of Angels."

Bosch remembered that Hollywood ran its homicide squad in three-man teams instead of the traditional partnerships.

"Any chance the three-bagger is connected to this?"

He pointed to the gathering of technicians around the body on the overlook.

"No, that's a straight gang shoot-'em-up," Edgar said. "I think this thing is a whole different ball game and I'm happy for you to take it."

"Good," Bosch said. "I'll cut you loose as soon as I can. Anybody look in the car yet?"

"Not really. Waiting on you."

"Okay. Anybody go to the victim's house on Arrowhead?"

"No on that, too."

"Anybody knock on any doors?"

"Not yet. We were working the scene first."

Edgar obviously had decided early that the case would be passed to RHD. It bothered

Bosch that nothing had been done but at the same time, he knew it would be his and Ferras's to work fresh from the start, and that wasn't a bad thing. There was a long history in the department of cases getting damaged or bungled while in transition from divisional to downtown detective teams.

He looked at the lighted clearing and counted a total of five men working on or near the body for the forensics and coroner's teams.

"Well," he said, "since you're working the crime scene first, did anybody look for foot impressions around the body before you let the techs approach?"

Bosch couldn't keep the tone of annoyance out of his voice.

"Harry," Edgar said, his tone now showing annoyance with Bosch's annoyance, "a couple hundred people stand around on this overlook every damn day. We coulda been looking at footprints till Christmas if we'd wanted to take the time. I didn't think we did. We had a body lying out here in a public place and needed to get to it. Besides that, it looks like a professional hit. That means the shoes, the gun, the car, everything's already long gone by now."

Bosch nodded. He wanted to dismiss this and move on.

"Okay," he said evenly, "then I guess you're clear."

Edgar nodded and Bosch thought he might be embarrassed.

"Like I said, Harry, I didn't expect it to be you."

Meaning he would not have dogged it for Harry, only for somebody else from RHD.

"Sure," Bosch said. "I understand."

After Edgar left, Bosch went back to his car and got the Maglite out of the trunk. He walked back to the Porsche, put on gloves and opened the driver-side door. He leaned into the car and looked around. On the passenger seat was a briefcase. It was unlocked and when he popped the snaps it opened to reveal several files, a calculator and various pads, pens and papers. He closed it and left it in its place. Its position on the seat told him that the victim had likely arrived at the overlook by himself. He had met his killer here. He had not brought his killer with him. This, Bosch thought, might be significant.

He opened the glove box next and several more clip-on IDs like the one found on the body fell to the floorboard. He picked them up one by one and saw that each access badge had been issued by a different local hospital. But the swipe cards all bore the same name and photo. Stanley Kent, the man (Bosch presumed) who was lying dead in the clearing.

He noticed that on the back of several of the tags there were handwritten notations. He looked at these for a long moment. Most were numbers with the letters *L* or *R* at the end and he concluded that they were lock combinations.

Bosch looked farther into the glove box and found even more IDs and access key cards. As far as he could tell, the dead man—if he was Stanley Kent—had clearance access to just about every hospital in Los Angeles County. He also had the combinations to security locks at almost every one of the hospitals. Bosch briefly considered that the IDs and key cards might be counterfeits used by the victim in some sort of hospital scam.

Bosch returned everything to the glove box and closed it. He then looked under and between the seats and found nothing of interest. He backed out of the car and went to the open trunk.

The trunk was small and empty. But in the beam of his flashlight he noted that there were four indentations in the carpet lining the bottom. It was clear that something square and heavy with four legs or wheels had been carried in the trunk. Because the trunk was found in the open position it was likely that the object—whatever it was—had been taken during the killing.

"Detective?"

Bosch turned and put the beam of his light into the face of a patrolman. It was the officer who had taken his name and badge number at the perimeter. He lowered the light.

"What is it?"

"There's an FBI agent here. She's asking permission to enter the crime scene."

"Where is she?"

The officer led the way back to the yellow tape. As Bosch got close he saw a woman standing next to the open door of a car. She was alone and she wasn't smiling. Bosch felt the thud of uneasy recognition hit his chest.

"Hello, Harry," she said when she saw him.

"Hello, Rachel," he said.

TWO

It had been almost six months since he had seen Special Agent Rachel Walling of the Federal Bureau of Investigation. As he approached her at the tape, Bosch was sure that not a day had gone by in that time when he hadn't thought about her. He had never imagined, however, that they would be reunited—if they ever were reunited—in the middle of the night at a murder scene. She was dressed in jeans, an oxford shirt and a dark blue blazer. Her dark hair was unkempt but she still looked beautiful. She obviously had been called in from home, just as Bosch had. She wasn't smiling and Bosch was reminded of how badly things had ended the last time.

"Look," he said, "I know I've been ignoring you but you didn't have to go to all the trouble of tracking me down at a crime scene just to—"

"It's not really a time for humor," she said, cutting him off. "If this is what I think it might be."

They'd last had contact on the Echo Park case. He had found her at the time working for a shadowy FBI unit called Tactical Intelligence. She had never explained what exactly the unit did and Bosch had never pushed it, since it wasn't important to the Echo Park investigation. He had reached out to her because of her past tenure as a profiler—and their past personal history. The Echo Park case had gone sideways and so had any chance for another romance. As Bosch looked at her now, he knew she was all business and he had a feeling he was about to find out what the Tactical Intelligence Unit was all about.

"What is it you think it might be?" he asked.

"I'll tell you when I can tell you. Can I please see the scene?"

Reluctantly, Bosch lifted the crime scene tape and returned her perfunctory attitude with his standard sarcasm.

"Come on in, then, Agent Walling," he said. "Why don't you just make yourself at home?"

She stepped under and stopped, at least respecting his right to lead her to his crime scene.

"I actually might be able to help you here," she said. "If I can see the body I might be able to make a formal identification for you."

She held up a file that she had been carrying down at her side.

"This way, then," Bosch said.

He led her to the clearing, where the victim was cast in the sterilizing fluorescent light from the mobile units. The dead man was lying on the orange dirt about five feet from the drop-off at the edge of the overlook. Beyond the body and over the edge the moonlight reflected off the reservoir below. Past the dam the city spread out in a blanket of a million lights. The cool evening air made the lights shimmer like floating dreams.

Bosch put out his arm to stop Walling at the edge of the light circle. The victim had been rolled over by the medical examiner and was now faceup. There were abrasions on the dead man's face and forehead but Bosch thought he could recognize the man in the photos on the hospital tags in the glove box. Stanley Kent. His shirt was open, exposing a hairless chest of pale white skin. There was an incision mark on one side of the torso where the medical examiner had pushed a temperature probe into the liver.

"Evening, Harry," said Joe Felton, the medical examiner. "Or I guess I should say, good morning. Who's your friend there? I thought they teamed you with Iggy Ferras."

"I am with Ferras," Bosch responded. "This is Special Agent Walling from the FBI's Tactical Intelligence Unit."

"Tactical Intelligence? What will they think of next?"

"I think it's one of those Homeland Security–type operations. You know, don't ask, don't tell, that sort of thing. She says she might be able to confirm an ID for us."

Walling gave Bosch a look that told him he was being juvenile.

"All right if we come in, Doc?" Bosch asked.

"Sure, Harry, we're pretty much squared away here."

Bosch started to step forward but Walling moved quickly in front of him and walked into the harsh light. Without hesitation she took a position over the body. She opened the file and took out a color 8 x 10 face shot. She bent down and held it next to the dead man's face. Bosch stepped in close at her side to make a comparison himself.

"It's him," she said. "Stanley Kent."

Bosch nodded his agreement and then offered his hand to her so that she could step back over the body. She ignored it and did it without help. Bosch looked down at Felton, who was squatting next to the body.

"So, Doc, you want to tell us what we've got here?"

Bosch stooped down on the other side of the body to get a better look.

"We've got a man who was brought here or came here for whatever reason and was made to get down on his knees."

Felton pointed to the victim's pants. There were smudges of orange dirt on both knees.

"Then somebody shot him twice in the back of the head and he went down face first. The facial injuries you see came when he hit the ground. He was already dead by then."

Bosch nodded.

"No exit wounds," Felton added. "Probably something small like a twenty-two with the ricochet effect inside the skull. Very efficient."

Bosch realized now that Lieutenant Gandle had been speaking figuratively when he mentioned that the victim's brains had been blown across the view from the overlook. He would have to remember Gandle's tendency toward hyperbole in the future.

"Time of death?" he asked Felton.

"Going by the liver temp I would say four or five hours," the medical examiner replied. "Eight o'clock, give or take."

That last part troubled Bosch. He knew that by eight it would have been dark and all the sunset worshippers would have been long gone. But the two shots would have echoed from the overlook and into the houses on the nearby bluffs. Yet no one had made a call to the police, and the body wasn't found until a patrol car happened by three hours later.

"I know what you are thinking," Felton said. "What about the sound? There is a possible explanation. Guys, let's roll him back over."

Bosch stood up and stepped out of the

way while Felton and one of his assistants turned the body over. Bosch glanced at Walling and for a moment their eyes locked, until she looked back down at the body.

Turning the body had exposed the bullet entry wounds in the back of the head. The victim's black hair was matted with blood. The back of his white shirt was spattered with a fine spray of a brown substance that immediately drew Bosch's attention. He had been to too many crime scenes to remember or count. He didn't think that was blood on the dead man's shirt.

"That's not blood, is it?"

"No, it's not," Felton said. "I think we'll find out from the lab that it's good old Coca-Cola syrup. The residue you might find in the bottom of an empty bottle or can."

Before Bosch could respond Walling did.

"An improvised silencer to dampen the sound of the shots," she said. "You tape an empty plastic liter Coke bottle to the muzzle of the weapon and the sound of the shot is significantly reduced as sound waves are projected into the bottle rather than the open air. If the bottle had a residue of Coke in it, the liquid would be spattered onto the target of the shot."

Felton looked at Bosch and nodded ap-
provingly.

"Where'd you get her, Harry? She's a
keeper."

Bosch looked at Walling. He, too, was impressed.

"Internet," she said.

Bosch nodded though he didn't believe
her.

"And there is one other thing you should
note," Felton said, drawing attention back to
the body.

Bosch stooped down again. Felton reached
across the body to point at the hand on
Bosch's side.

"We have one of these on each hand."

He was pointing to a red plastic ring on
the middle finger. Bosch looked at it and then
checked the other hand. There was a matching red ring. On the inside of each hand the
ring had a white facing that looked like some
sort of tape.

"What are they?" Bosch asked.

"I don't know yet," Felton said. "But I
think—"

"I do," Walling said.

Bosch looked up at her. He nodded. Of
course she knew.

"They're called TLD rings," Walling said. "Stands for thermal luminescent dosimetry. It's an early-warning device. It's a ring that reads radiation exposure."

The news brought an eerie silence to the gathering. Until Walling continued.

"And I'll give you a tip," she said. "When they are turned inward like that, with the TLD screen on the inside of the hand, that usually means the wearer directly handles radioactive materials."

Bosch stood up.

"Okay, everybody," he ordered, "back away from the body. Everybody just back away."

The crime scene techs, the coroner's people and Bosch all started moving away from the body. But Walling didn't move. She raised her hands like she was calling for a congregation's attention in church.

"Hold on, hold on," she said. "Nobody has to back away. It's cool, it's cool. It's safe."

Everybody paused but nobody moved back to their original positions.

"If there was an exposure threat here, then the TLD screens on the rings would be black," she said. "That's the early warning. But they haven't turned black, so we're all safe. Additionally, I have this."

She pulled back her jacket to reveal a small black box clipped to her belt like a pager.

"Radiation monitor," she explained. "If we had a problem, believe me, this thing would be screaming bloody murder and I'd be running at the front of the pack. But we don't. Everything is cool here, okay?"

The people at the crime scene hesitantly started to return to their positions. Harry Bosch moved in close to Walling and took her by an elbow.

"Can we talk over here for a minute?"

They moved out of the clearing toward the curb at Mulholland. Bosch felt things shifting but tried not to show it. He was agitated. He didn't want to lose control of the crime scene, and this sort of information threatened to do just that.

"What are you doing here, Rachel?" he asked. "What's going on?"

"Just like you, I got a call in the middle of the night. I was told to roll out."

"That tells me nothing."

"I assure you that I am here to help."

"Then start by telling me exactly what you are doing here and who sent you out. That would help me a lot."

Walling looked around and then back at
Bosch. She pointed out beyond the yellow
tape.

"Can we?"

Bosch held out his hand, telling her to lead
the way. They went under the tape and out
into the street. When he judged that they
were out of earshot of everyone else at the
crime scene, Bosch stopped and looked at
her.

"Okay, this is far enough," he said. "What
is going on here? Who called you out here?"

She locked eyes with him again.

"Listen, what I tell you here has to remain
confidential," she said. "For now."

"Look, Rachel, I don't have time for—"

"Stanley Kent is on a list. When you or one
of your colleagues ran his name on the National Crime Index Computer tonight a flag
went up in Washington, DC, and a call went
out to me at Tactical."

"What, was he a terrorist?"

"No, he was a medical physicist. And, as
far as I know, a law-abiding citizen."

"Then what's with the radiation rings and
the FBI showing up in the middle of the night?
What list was Stanley Kent on?"

Walling ignored the question.

"Let me ask you something, Harry. Has anyone checked on this man's home or wife yet?"

"Not yet. We were working the crime scene first. I plan to—"

"Then I think we need to do that right now," she said in an urgent tone. "You can ask your questions along the way. Get the guy's keys in case we need to go in. And I'll go get my car."

Walling started to move away but Bosch caught her by the arm.

"I'm driving," he said.

He pointed toward his Mustang and left her there. He headed to the patrol car, where the evidence bags were still spread on the trunk. As he made his way he regretted having already cut Edgar loose from the scene. He signaled the watch sergeant over.

"Listen, I have to leave the scene to check on the victim's house. I shouldn't be gone long and Detective Ferras should be here any minute. Just maintain the scene until one of us gets here."

"You got it."

Bosch pulled out his cell phone and called his partner.

"Where are you?"

"I just cleared Parker Center. I'm twenty minutes away."

Bosch explained that he was leaving the scene and that Ferras needed to hurry. He disconnected, grabbed the evidence bag containing the key ring off the cruiser's trunk and shoved it into his coat pocket.

As he got to his car he saw Walling already in the passenger seat. She was finishing a call and closing her cell phone.

"Who was that?" Bosch asked after getting in. "The president?"

"My partner," she replied. "I told him to meet me at the house. Where's your partner?"

"He's coming."

Bosch started the car. As soon as they pulled out he began asking questions.

"If Stanley Kent wasn't a terrorist, then what list was he on?"

"As a medical physicist he had direct access to radioactive materials. That put him on a list."

Bosch thought of all the hospital name tags he had found in the dead man's Porsche.

"Access where? In the hospitals?"

"Exactly. That's where it's kept. These are

materials primarily used in the treatment of cancer."

Bosch nodded. He was getting the picture but still didn't have enough information.

"Okay, so what am I missing here, Rachel? Lay it out for me."

"Stanley Kent had direct access to materials that some people in the world would like to get their hands on. Materials that could be very, very valuable to these other people. But not in the treatment of cancer."

"Terrorists."

"Exactly."

"Are you saying that this guy could just waltz into a hospital and get this stuff? Aren't there regulations?"

Walling nodded.

"There are always regulations, Harry. But just having them is not always enough. Repetition, routine—these are the cracks in any security system. We used to leave the cockpit doors on commercial airlines unlocked. Now we don't. It takes an event of life-altering consequences to change procedures and strengthen precautions. Do you understand what I am saying?"

He thought of the notations on the back of some of the ID cards in the victim's Porsche.

Could Stanley Kent have been so lax about the security of these materials that he wrote access combinations on the back of his ID cards? Bosch's instincts told him the answer was probably yes.

"I understand," he told Walling.

"So, then, if you were going to circumvent an existing security system, no matter how strong or weak, who would you go to?" she asked.

Bosch nodded.

"Somebody with intimate knowledge of that security system."

"Exactly."

Bosch turned onto Arrowhead Drive and started looking at address numbers on the curb.

"So you're saying this could be an event of life-altering consequences?"

"No, I'm not saying that. Not yet."

"Did you know Kent?"

Bosch looked at Walling as he asked and she looked surprised by the question. It had been a long shot but he threw it out there for the reaction, not necessarily the answer. Walling turned from him and looked out her window before answering. Bosch knew the move. A classic tell. He knew she would now lie to him.

"No, I never met the man."

Bosch pulled into the next driveway and stopped the car.

"What are you doing?" she asked.

"This is it. It's Kent's house."

They were in front of a house that had no lights on inside or out. It looked like no one lived there.

"No, it isn't," Walling said. "His house is down another block and—"

She stopped when she realized Bosch had smoked her out. Bosch stared at her for a moment in the dark car before speaking.

"You want to level with me now or do you want to get out of the car?"

"Look, Harry, I told you. There are things I can't—"

"Get out of the car, Agent Walling. I'll handle this myself."

"Look, you have to under—"

"This is a homicide. *My* homicide. Get out of the car."

She didn't move.

"I can make one phone call and you'd be removed from this investigation before you got back to the scene," she said.

"Then do it. I'd rather be kicked to the curb right now than be a mushroom for the feds.

Isn't that one of the bureau's slogans? Keep the locals in the dark and bury them in cow shit? Well, not me, not tonight and not on my own case."

He started to reach across her lap to open her door. Walling pushed him back and raised her hands in surrender.

"All right, all right," she said. "What is it you want to know?"

"I want the truth this time. All of it."

THREE

BOSCH TURNED IN HIS SEAT to look directly at Walling. He was not going to move the car until she started talking.

"You obviously knew who Stanley Kent was and where he lived," he said. "You lied to me. Now, was he a terrorist or not?"

"I told you, no, and that is the truth. He was a citizen. He was a physicist. He was on a watch list because he handled radioactive sources which could be used—in the wrong hands—to harm members of the public."

"What are you talking about? How would this happen?"

"Through exposure. And that could take many different forms. Individual assault—you remember last Thanksgiving the Russian who was dosed with polonium in London? That was a specific target attack, though there were ancillary victims as well. The material Kent had access to could also be used on a larger scale—a mall, a subway, whatever. It all depends on the quantity and, of course, the delivery device."

"Delivery device? Are you talking about a bomb? Somebody could make a dirty bomb with the stuff he handled?"

"In some applications, yes."

"I thought that was an urban legend, that there's never actually been a dirty bomb."

"The official designation is IED—improvised explosive device. And put it this way, it's only an urban legend until precisely the moment that the first one is detonated."

Bosch nodded and got back on track. He gestured to the house in front of them.

"How did you know this isn't the Kent house?"

Walling rubbed her forehead as though she were tired of his annoying questions and had a headache.

"Because I have been to his house before. Okay? Early last year my partner and I came to Kent's house and briefed him and his wife on the potential dangers of his profession. We did a security check on their home and told them to take precautions. We had been asked to do it by the Department of Homeland Security. Okay?"

"Yeah, okay. And was that routine for the Tactical Intelligence Unit and the Department of Homeland Security, or was that because there had been a threat to him?"

"Not a threat specifically aimed at him, no. Look, we're wasting—"

"Then to who? A threat to who?"

Walling adjusted her position in the seat and let her breath out in exasperation.

"There wasn't a threat to anyone specifically. We were simply taking precautions. Sixteen months ago someone entered a cancer clinic in Greensboro, North Carolina, circumvented elaborate security measures and removed twenty-two small tubes of a radioisotope called cesium one-thirty-seven. The legitimate medical use of this material in that setting was in the treatment of gynecological cancer. We don't know who got in there or why, but the material was taken. When news of the theft went out on the wire somebody in the Joint Terrorism Task Force here in L.A. thought it would be a good idea to assess the security of these materials in local hospitals and to warn those who have access to and handle the stuff to take precautions and to be alert. Can we *please* go now?"

"And that was you."

"*Yes.* You got it. It was the federal trickle-down theory at work. It fell to me and my partner to go out and talk to people like Stanley Kent. We met him and his wife at their house so we could do a security check of the place at the same time we told him that he should start watching his back. That is the same reason I was the one who got the call when his name came up on the flag."

Bosch dropped the transmission into reverse and pulled quickly out of the driveway.

"Why didn't you just tell me this up front?"

In the street the car jerked forward as Bosch threw it into drive.

"Because nobody got killed in Greensboro," Walling said defiantly. "This whole thing could be something different. I was told to approach with caution and discretion. I'm sorry I lied to you."

"A little late for that, Rachel. Did your people get the cesium back in Greensboro?"

She didn't answer.

"Did you?"

"No, not yet. The word is that it was sold on the black market. The material itself is quite valuable on a monetary basis, even if used in the proper medical context. That's why we are not sure what we've got here. That's why I was sent."

In ten more seconds they were at the correct block of Arrowhead Drive and Bosch started looking at address numbers again. But Walling directed him.

"That one up on the left, I think. With the black shutters. It's hard to tell in the dark."

Bosch pulled in and chunked the transmission into park before the car had stopped. He jumped out and headed to the front door. The house was dark. Not even the light over the door was lit. But as Bosch approached the front door he saw that it had been left ajar.

"It's open," he said.

Bosch and Walling drew their weapons. Bosch placed his hand on the door and slowly pushed it open. With guns up they entered the dark and quiet house and Bosch quickly swept the wall with his hand until he found a light switch.

The lights came on, revealing a living room that was neat but empty, with no sign of trouble.

"Mrs. Kent?" Walling called out loudly. Then to Bosch in a lower voice she said, "There's just his wife, no children."

Walling called out once more but the house remained silent. There was a hallway to the right and Bosch moved toward it. He found another light switch and illuminated a passageway with four closed doors and an alcove.

The alcove was a home office that was empty. He saw a blue reflection on the window that was cast by a computer screen. They passed by the alcove and went door by door clearing what looked like a guest bedroom and then a home gym with cardio machines and with workout mats hanging on the wall. The third door was to a guest bathroom that was empty and the fourth led to the master bedroom.

They entered the master and Bosch once

more flicked up a wall switch. They found Mrs. Kent.

She was on the bed naked, gagged and hog-tied with her hands behind her back. Her eyes were closed. Walling rushed to the bed to see if she was alive while Bosch moved through the bedroom to clear the bathroom and a walk-in closet. There was no one.

When he got back to the bed he saw that Walling had removed the gag and used a pocketknife to slice through the black plastic snap ties that had been used to bind the woman's wrists and ankles together behind her back. Rachel was pulling the bedspread over the unmoving woman's naked body. There was a distinct odor of urine in the room.

"Is she alive?" Bosch asked.

"She's alive. I think she's just passed out. She was left here like this."

Walling started rubbing the woman's wrists and hands. They had turned dark and almost purple from lack of blood circulation.

"Get help," she told him.

Annoyed with himself for not reacting until ordered, Bosch pulled out his phone and walked out into the hallway while he called the central communications center to get paramedics rolling.

"Ten minutes," he said after hanging up and coming back into the bedroom.

Bosch felt a wave of excitement go through him. They now had a live witness. The woman on the bed would be able to tell them at least something about what had happened. He knew that it would be vitally important to get her talking as soon as possible.

There was a loud groan as the woman regained consciousness.

"Mrs. Kent, it's okay," Walling said. "It's okay. You're safe now."

The woman tensed and her eyes widened when she saw the two strangers in front of her. Walling held up her credentials.

"FBI, Mrs. Kent. Do you remember me?"

"What? What is—where's my husband?"

She started to get up but then realized she was naked beneath the bedcovers and tried to pull them tightly around herself. Her fingers were apparently still numb and couldn't find purchase. Walling helped pull the spread around her.

"Where is Stanley?"

Walling knelt at the bottom of the bed so

that she was on an equal level with her. She looked up at Bosch as if seeking direction on how to handle the woman's question.

"Mrs. Kent, your husband is not here," Bosch said. "I am Detective Bosch with the LAPD and this is Agent Walling with the FBI. We're trying to find out what happened to your husband."

The woman looked up at Bosch and then at Walling and her eyes held on the federal agent.

"I remember you," she said. "You came to the house to warn us. Is that what is happening? Do the men who were here have Stanley?"

Rachel leaned in close and spoke in a calming voice.

"Mrs. Kent, we—it's Alicia, right? Alicia, we need for you to calm down a little bit so that we can talk and possibly help you. Would you like to get dressed?"

Alicia Kent nodded.

"Okay, we'll give you some space here," Walling said. "You get dressed and we'll wait for you in the living room. First let me ask, have you been injured in any way?"

The woman shook her head.

"Are you sure . . . ?"

Walling didn't finish, as though she were intimidated by her own question. Bosch wasn't. He knew they needed to know precisely what had happened here.

"Mrs. Kent, were you sexually assaulted here tonight?"

The woman shook her head again.

"They made me take off my clothes. That was all they did."

Bosch studied her eyes, hoping to read them and be able to tell if she was telling a lie.

"Okay," Walling said, interrupting the moment. "We'll leave you to get dressed. When the paramedics arrive we will still want them to check you for injuries."

"I'll be fine," Alicia Kent said. "What happened to my husband?"

"We're not sure what's happened," Bosch said. "You get dressed and come out to the living room, then we'll tell you what we know."

Clutching the bedspread around herself, she tentatively stood up from the bed. Bosch saw the stain on the mattress and knew that Alicia Kent had either been so scared during her ordeal that she had urinated or the wait for rescue had been too long.

She took one step toward the closet and appeared to be falling over. Bosch moved in and grabbed her before she fell.

"Are you all right?"

"I'm fine. I think I'm just a little dizzy. What time is it?"

Bosch looked at the digital clock on the right-side bed table but its screen was blank. It was turned off or unplugged. He turned his right wrist without letting go of her and looked at his watch.

"It's almost one in the morning."

Her body seemed to tighten in his grasp.

"Oh, my God!" she cried. "It's been hours—where is Stanley?"

Bosch moved his hands to her shoulders and helped her stand up straight.

"You get dressed and we'll talk about it," he said.

She walked unsteadily to the closet and opened the door. A full-length mirror was attached to the outside of the door. Her opening it swung Bosch's reflection back at him. In the moment, he thought that maybe he saw something new in his eyes. Something not there when he had checked himself in the mirror before leaving his house. A look of discomfort, perhaps even a fear of the unknown. It was understandable, he decided. He had worked a thousand murder cases in his time, but never one that had taken him in the direction he was now traveling. Maybe fear was appropriate.

Alicia Kent took a white terry-cloth robe off a hook on a wall inside the closet and carried it with her to the bathroom. She left the closet door open and Bosch had to look away from his own reflection.

Walling headed out of the bedroom and Bosch followed.

"What do you think?" she asked as she moved down the hall.

"I think we're lucky to have a witness," Bosch replied. "She'll be able to tell us what happened."

"Hopefully."

Bosch decided to make another survey of the house while waiting for Alicia Kent to get dressed. This time he checked the back-yard and the garage as well as every room again. He found nothing amiss, though he did note that the two-car garage was empty. If the Kents had another car in addition to the Porsche, then it wasn't on the prem-ises.

Following the walk-through he stood in the

backyard looking up at the Hollywood sign and calling central communications again to ask that a second forensics team be dispatched to process the Kent house. He also checked on the ETA of the paramedics coming to examine Alicia Kent and was told that they were still five minutes away. This was ten minutes after he had been told that they were ten minutes away.

Next he called Lieutenant Gandle, waking him at his home. His supervisor listened quietly as Bosch updated him. The federal involvement and the rising possibility of a terrorism angle to the investigation gave Gandle pause.

"Well . . . ," he said when Bosch was finished. "It looks like I will have to wake some people up."

He meant he was going to have to send word up the department ladder of the case and the larger dimensions it was taking on. The last thing an RHD lieutenant would want or need would be to get called into the OCP in the morning and asked why he hadn't alerted command staff earlier to the case and its growing implications. Bosch knew that Gandle would now act to protect himself as well as to seek direction from

above. This was fine with Bosch and expected. But it gave him pause as well. The
LAPD had its own Office of Homeland Security. It was commanded by a man most
people in the department viewed as a loose
cannon who was unqualified and unsuited
for the job.

"Is one of those wake-ups going to Captain Hadley?" Bosch asked.

Captain Don Hadley was the twin brother
of James Hadley, who happened to be a
member of the Police Commission, the politically appointed panel with LAPD oversight
and the authority to appoint and retain the
chief of police. Less than a year after James
Hadley was placed on the commission by
mayoral appointment and the approval of the
city council, his twin brother jumped from being second in command of the Valley Traffic
Division to being commander of the newly
formed Office of Homeland Security. This
was seen at the time as a political move by
the then–chief of police, who was desper-
ately trying to keep his job. It didn't work. He
was fired and a new chief appointed. But in
the transition Hadley kept his job command-
ing the OHS.

The mission of the OHS was to interface

with federal agencies and maintain a flow of intelligence data. In the last six years Los Angeles had been targeted by terrorists at least two times that were known. In each incident the LAPD found out about the threat after it had been foiled by the feds. This was embarrassing to the department, and the OHS had been formed so that the LAPD could make intelligence inroads and eventually know what the federal government knew about its own backyard.

The problem was that in practice it was largely suspected that the LAPD remained shut out by the feds. And in order to hide this failing and to justify his position and unit, Captain Hadley had taken to holding grandstanding press conferences and showing up with his black-clad OHS unit at any crime scene where there was a remote possibility of terrorist involvement. An overturned tanker truck on the Hollywood Freeway brought the OHS out in force until it was determined that the tanker was carrying milk. A shooting of a rabbi at a temple in Westwood brought the same response until the incident was determined to have been the product of a love triangle.

And so it went. After about the fourth misfire, the commander of the OHS was baptized with a new name among the rank and file. Captain Don Hadley became known as Captain Done Badly. But he remained in his position, thanks to the thin veil of politics that hung over his appointment. The last Bosch had heard about Hadley through the department grapevine was that he had put his entire squad back into the academy for training in urban assault tactics.

"I don't know about Hadley," Gandle said in response to Bosch. "He'll probably be looped in. I'll start with my captain and he'll make the call on who gets the word from there. But that's not your concern, Harry. You do your job and don't worry about Hadley. The people you have to watch your back with are the feds."

"Got it."

"Remember, with the feds it's always time to worry when they start telling you just what you want to hear."

Bosch nodded. The advice followed a time-honored LAPD tradition of distrusting the FBI. And, of course, it was a tradition honored for just as long by the FBI in terms of distrusting the LAPD right back. It was the reason the OHS was born.

When Bosch came back into the house he found Walling on her cell phone and a man he had never seen before standing in the living room. He was tall, midforties and he exuded that undeniable FBI confidence Bosch had seen many times before. The man put out his hand.

"You must be Detective Bosch," he said. "Jack Brenner. Rachel's my partner."

Bosch shook his hand. The way he said Rachel was his partner was a small thing but it told Bosch a lot. There was something proprietary about it. Brenner was telling him that the senior partner was now on the job, whether that would be Rachel's view of it or not.

"So, you two have met."

Bosch turned. Walling was off the phone now.

"Sorry," she said. "I was filling in the special agent in charge. He's decided to devote all of Tactical to this. He's running out three teams to start hitting the hospitals to see if Kent has been in any of the hot labs today."

"The hot lab is where they keep the radioactive stuff?" Bosch asked.

"Yes. Kent had access through security to

just about all of them in the county. We have to figure out if he was inside any of them today."

Bosch knew that he could probably narrow the search down to one medical facility. Saint Agatha's Clinic for Women. Kent was wearing an ID tag from the hospital when he was murdered. Walling and Brenner didn't know that but Bosch decided not to tell them yet. He sensed the investigation was moving away from him and he wanted to hold on to what might be the one piece of inside information he still had.

"What about the LAPD?" he asked instead.

"The LAPD?" Brenner said, jumping on the question ahead of Walling. "You mean what about you, Bosch? Is that what you're asking?"

"Yeah, that's right. Where do I stand in this?"

Brenner spread his hands in a gesture of openness.

"Don't worry, you're in. You're with us all the way."

The federal agent nodded like it was a promise as good as gold.

"Good," Bosch said. "That's just what I wanted to hear."

He looked at Walling for confirmation of her partner's statement. But she looked away.

FOUR

WHEN ALICIA KENT FINALLY CAME OUT of the
master bedroom she had brushed her hair
and washed her face but had put on only the
white robe. Bosch now saw how attractive
she was. Small and dark and exotic-looking
in some way. He guessed that taking her
husband's name had hidden a bloodline from
somewhere far away. Her black hair had a
luminescent quality to it. It framed an olive
face that was beautiful and sorrowful at the
same time.

She noticed Brenner and he nodded and
introduced himself. Alicia Kent seemed so

dazed by what was happening that she showed no recognition of Brenner in the way that she had remembered Walling. Brenner directed her to the couch and told her to sit down.

"Where is my husband?" she demanded, this time with a voice that was stronger and calmer than before. "I want to know what is going on."

Rachel sat down next to her, ready to console if necessary. Brenner took a chair near the fireplace. Bosch remained standing. He never liked to be sitting down all cozy when he delivered this sort of news.

"Mrs. Kent," Bosch said, taking the lead in a proprietary effort to keep his hold of the case. "I am a homicide detective. I am here because earlier tonight we found the body of a man we believe to be your husband. I am very sorry to tell you this."

Her head dropped forward as she received the news, then her hands came up and they covered her face. A shudder went through her body and the sound of a helpless moan came from behind her hands. Then she started to cry, deep sobs that shook her shoulders so much that she had to lower her hands to hold the robe from coming open. Walling reached over and put a hand on the back of her neck.

Brenner offered to get her a glass of water and she nodded. While he was gone Bosch studied the woman and saw the tears streaking her cheeks. It was dirty work, telling someone that their loved one was dead. He had done it hundreds of times but it wasn't something you ever got used to or even good at. It had also been done to him. When his own mother was murdered more than forty years before, he got the news from a cop just after he climbed out of a swimming pool at a youth hall. His response was to jump back in and try to never come back up.

Brenner delivered the water, and the brand-new widow drank half of it down. Before anyone could ask a question there was a knock on the door and Bosch stepped over and let in two paramedics carrying big equipment boxes. Bosch moved out of the way while they came forward to assess the woman's physical condition. He signaled Walling and Brenner into the kitchen, where they could confer in whispers. He realized that they should have talked about this earlier.

"So how do you want to handle her?" Bosch asked.

Brenner spread his hands wide again as though he was open to suggestions. It appeared to be his signature gesture.

"I think you keep the lead," the agent said. "We'll step in when needed. If you don't like that we could—"

"No, that's good. I'll keep the lead."

He looked at Walling, waiting for an objection, but she was fine with it, too. He turned to leave the kitchen but Brenner stopped him.

"Bosch, I want to be up front with you," Brenner said.

Bosch turned back.

"Meaning?"

"Meaning I had you checked out. The word is you—"

"What do you mean you checked me out? You asked questions about me?"

"I needed to know who we're working with. All I knew about you prior to this is what I'd heard about Echo Park. I wanted—"

"If you have any questions you can ask me."

Brenner raised his hands, palms out.

"Fair enough."

Bosch left the kitchen and stood in the living room, waiting for the paramedics to finish with Alicia Kent. One of the medical men was putting some sort of cream on the chafe marks on her wrists and ankles. The other was taking a blood-pressure reading. Bosch saw that bandages had been placed on her neck and one wrist, apparently covering wounds that he hadn't noticed before.

His phone buzzed and Bosch went back into the kitchen to take the call. He noticed that Walling and Brenner were gone, apparently having slipped into another part of the house. It made Bosch anxious. He didn't know what they were looking for or up to.

The call was from his partner. Ferras had finally made it to the crime scene.

"Is the body still there?" Bosch asked.

"No, the ME just cleared the scene," Ferras said. "I think Forensics is finishing up, too."

Bosch updated him on the direction the case appeared to be going, telling him about the federal involvement and the potentially dangerous materials Stanley Kent had had access to. He then directed him to start knocking on doors and looking for witnesses who might have seen or heard something relating to the killing of Stanley Kent. He knew it was a long shot, because no one had called 9-1-1 after the shooting.

"Should I do that now, Harry? It's the middle of the night and people are slee—"

"Yes, Ignacio, you should do it now."

Bosch wasn't worried about waking people up. There was a good chance that the generator that powered the crime scene lights had awakened the neighborhood anyway. But the canvassing of the neighborhood had to be done and it was always better to find witnesses sooner rather than later.

When Bosch came out of the kitchen the paramedics had packed up and were leaving. They told Bosch that Alicia Kent was physically fine, with minor wounds and skin abrasions. They also said they had given her a pill to help calm her and a tube of the cream to continue to apply to the chafe marks on her wrists and ankles.

Walling was sitting on the couch next to her again and Brenner was back in his seat by the fireplace.

Bosch sat down on the chair directly across the glass coffee table from Alicia Kent.

"Mrs. Kent," he began, "we are very sorry for your loss and the trauma you have been through. But it is very urgent that we move quickly with the investigation. In a perfect world we would wait until you were ready to talk to us. But it's not a perfect world. You know that better than we do now. We need to ask you questions about what happened here tonight."

She folded her arms across her chest and nodded that she understood.

"Then let's get started," Bosch said. "Can you tell us what happened?"

"Two men," she responded tearfully. "I never saw them. I mean their faces. I never saw their faces. There was a knock at the door and I answered. There was no one there. Then when I started to close the door they were there. They jumped out. They had on masks and hoods — like a sweat-shirt with a hood. They pushed their way in and they grabbed me. They had a knife and one of them grabbed me and held it against my throat. He told me he would cut my throat if I didn't do exactly what he told me to do."

She lightly touched the bandage on her neck.

"Do you remember what time this was?" Bosch asked.

"It was almost six o'clock," she said. "It had been dark for a while and I was about to start dinner. Stanley comes home most nights at seven. Unless he's working down in the South County or up in the desert."

The reminder of her husband's habits brought a new rush of tears into Alicia Kent's eyes and voice. Bosch tried to keep her on point by moving to the next question. He thought he already detected a slowing down of her speech. The pill the paramedics gave her was taking effect.

"What did the men do, Mrs. Kent?" he asked.

"They took me to the bedroom. They made me sit down on the bed and take off all my clothes. Then they—one of them—started to ask me questions. I was scared. I guess I got hysterical and he slapped me and he yelled at me. He told me to calm down and answer his questions."

"What did he ask you?"

"I can't remember everything. I was so scared."

"Try, Mrs. Kent. It's important. It will help us find your husband's killers."

"He asked me if we had a gun and he asked me where the—"

"Wait a minute, Mrs. Kent," Bosch said. "Let's go one at a time. He asked you if you had a gun. What did you tell him?"

"I was scared. I said, yes, we had a gun. He asked where it was and I told him it was in the drawer by the bed on my husband's side. It was the gun we got after you warned us about the dangers Stan faced with his job."

She said this last part while looking directly at Walling.

"Weren't you afraid that they would kill you with it?" Bosch asked. "Why did you tell them where the gun was?"

Alicia Kent looked down at her hands.

"I was sitting there naked. I was already sure they were going to rape me and kill me. I guess I thought it didn't matter anymore."

Bosch nodded as if he understood.

"What else did they ask you, Mrs. Kent?"

"They wanted to know where the keys to the car were. I told them. I told them everything they wanted to know."

"Is that your car they were talking about?"

"Yes, my car. In the garage. I keep the keys on the kitchen counter."

"I checked the garage. It's empty."

"I heard the garage door—after they were here. They must've taken the car."

Brenner abruptly stood up.

"We need to get this out," he interjected. "Can you tell us what kind of car it is and the license plate number?"

"It's a Chrysler Three Hundred. I can't remember the number. I could look it up in our insurance file."

Brenner held his hands up to stop her from getting up.

"Not necessary. I'll be able to get it. I'm going to call it in right away."

He got up to go to the kitchen to make the call without disturbing the interview. Bosch went back to his questions.

"What else did they ask you, Mrs. Kent?"

"They wanted our camera. The camera that worked with my husband's computer. I told them Stanley had a camera that I thought was in his desk. Whenever I answered a question, one man—the one who asked them—would then translate to the other, and then that man left the room. I guess he went to get the camera."

Now Walling stood up and headed toward the hallway leading to the bedrooms.

"Rachel, don't touch anything," Bosch said. "I have a crime scene team coming."

Walling waved as she disappeared down the hall. Brenner then came back into the room and nodded to Bosch.

"The BOLO's out," he said.

Alicia Kent asked what a BOLO was.

"It means 'be on the lookout,'" Bosch explained. "They'll be looking for your car. What happened next with the two men, Mrs. Kent?"

She grew tearful again as she answered.

"They . . . they tied me in that awful way and gagged me with one of my husband's neckties. Then after the one came back in with the camera, the other took a picture of me like that."

Bosch noted the look of burning humiliation on her face.

"He took a photograph?"

"Yes, that's all. Then they both left the room. The one who spoke English bent down and whispered that my husband would come to rescue me. Then he left."

That brought a long space of silence before Bosch continued.

"After they left the bedroom, did they leave the house right away?" he asked.

The woman shook her head.

"I heard them talking for a little while, then I heard the garage door. It rumbles in the house like an earthquake. I felt it twice — it opened and closed. After that I thought they were gone."

Brenner cut into the interview again.

"When I was in the kitchen I think I heard you say that one of the men translated for the other. Do you know what language they were speaking?"

Bosch was annoyed with Brenner for jumping in. He intended to ask about the language the intruders used but was carefully covering one aspect of the interview at a time. He had found in previous cases that it worked best with traumatized victims.

"I am not sure. The one who spoke in English had an accent but I don't know where it was from. I think Middle Eastern. I think when they spoke to each other it was Arabic or something. It was foreign, very guttural. But I don't know the different languages."

Brenner nodded as if her answer was confirming something.

"Do you remember anything else about what the men might have asked you or said in English?" Bosch asked.

"No, that's all."

"You said they wore masks. What kind of masks?"

She thought for a moment before answering.

"The pullover kind. Like you see robbers put on in movies or people wear for skiing."

"A wool ski mask."

She nodded.

"Yes, exactly."

"Okay, were they the kind with one hole for both eyes or was there a separate hole for each eye."

"Um, separate, I think. Yes, separate."

"Was there an opening for the mouth?"

"Uh . . . yes, there was. I remember watching the man's mouth when he spoke in the other language. I was trying to understand him."

"That's good, Mrs. Kent. You're being very helpful. What haven't I asked you?"

"I don't understand."

"What detail do you remember that I haven't asked you for?"

She thought about it and then shook her head.

"I don't know. I think I've told you everything I can remember."

Bosch wasn't convinced. He began to go through the story with her again, coming at the same information from new angles. It was a tried-and-true interview technique for eliciting new details and it did not fail him. The most interesting bit of new information to emerge in the second telling was that the man who spoke English also asked her what the password was to her e-mail account.

"Why would he want that?" Bosch asked.

"I don't know," Alicia Kent said. "I didn't ask. I just gave them what they wanted."

Near the end of the second telling of her ordeal the forensics team arrived and Bosch called for a break in the questioning. While Alicia Kent remained on the couch, he walked the tech team back to the master bedroom so they could start there. He then stepped into a corner of the room and called his partner. Ferras reported that he had found nobody so far who had seen or heard anything on the overlook. Bosch told him that when he wanted a break from knocking on doors he should check into Stanley Kent's ownership of a gun. They needed to find the make and model. It was looking like his own gun was probably the weapon he was killed with.

As Bosch closed the phone Walling called to him from the home office. Harry found her and Brenner standing behind the desk and looking at a computer screen.

"Look at this," Walling said.

"I told you," he said, "you shouldn't be touching anything yet."

"We don't have the luxury of time anymore," Brenner said. "Look at this."

Bosch came around the desk to look at the computer.

"Her e-mail account was left open," Walling said. "I went into the sent mail file. And this was sent to her husband's e-mail at six-twenty-one p.m. last night."

She clicked a button and opened up the e-mail that had been sent from Alicia Kent's account to her husband's. The subject line said

HOME EMERGENCY:
READ IMMEDIATELY!

Embedded in the body of the e-mail was a photograph of Alicia Kent naked and hogtied on the bed. The impact of the photo would be obvious to anyone, not just a husband.

Below the photograph was a message:

We have your wife. Retrieve for us
all cesium sources available to you.
Bring them in safe containment to the
Mulholland overlook near your home
by eight o'clock. We will be watching
you. If you tell anyone or make a call
we will know. The consequence will be
your wife being raped, tortured and left
in to many pieces to count. Use all
precautions while handling sources. Do
not be late or we will kill her.

Bosch read the message twice and believed he felt the same terror Stanley Kent
must have felt.

"'We will be watching . . . we will know . . .
we will kill her,'" Walling said. "No contrac-
tions. The 'too' in 'too many pieces' is spelled
wrong and then the odd construction of some
of the sentences. I don't think this was writ-
ten by someone whose original language is
English."

As she said it Bosch saw it and knew that
she was right.

"They send the message right from
here," Brenner said. "The husband gets it

at the office or on his PDA—did he have a PDA?"

Bosch had no expertise in this area. He hesitated.

"A personal digital assistant," Walling prompted. "You know, like a Palm Pilot or a phone with all the gadgets."

Bosch nodded.

"I think so," he said. "There was a Black-Berry cell phone recovered. It looks like it has a mini-keyboard."

"That works," Brenner said. "So no matter where he is, he gets this message and can probably view the photo, too."

All three of them were quiet while the impact of the e-mail registered. Finally, Bosch spoke, feeling guilty now about holding back earlier.

"I just remembered something. There was an ID tag on the body. From Saint Aggy's up in the Valley."

Brenner's eyes took on a sharpness.

"You just remembered a key piece of information like that?" he asked angrily.

"That's right. I for—"

"It doesn't matter now," Walling interjected. "Saint Aggy's is a women's cancer clinic. Cesium is used almost exclusively for treating cervical and uterine cancer."

Bosch nodded.

"Then we better get going," he said.

FIVE

Saint Agatha's Clinic for Women was in Syl-
mar at the north end of the San Fernando
Valley. Because it was the dead of night they
were making good time on the 170 Freeway
up. Bosch was behind the wheel of his Mustang, one eye on the fuel needle. He knew
he was going to need gas before coming
back down into the city. It was he and Brenner
in the car. It had been decided—by
Brenner—that Walling should stay behind
with Alicia Kent, to continue both questioning
and calming her. Walling didn't seem happy
about the assignment but Brenner, asserting

his seniority in the partnership, didn't give her room to debate it.

Brenner spent most of the drive taking and making a series of cell calls to and from superiors and fellow agents. It was clear to Bosch from the side of things he was able to hear that the big federal machine was gearing up for battle. A greater alarm had now been sounded. The e-mail sent to Stanley Kent had brought things into better focus and what was once a federal curiosity had now gone completely off the scale.

When Brenner finally closed the phone and put it back in his jacket pocket he turned slightly in his seat and looked over at Bosch.

"I've got a RAT team heading to Saint Aggy's," he said. "They'll go into the materials safe to check it out."

"A rat team?"

"Radiological-attack team."

"What's their ETA?"

"Didn't ask but they might beat us. They've got a chopper."

Bosch was impressed. It meant that there had been a rapid-response team on duty somewhere in the middle of the night. He thought about how he had been awake and waiting for the call out that night. The members of the radiological-attack team must wait for the call they hope never comes. He remembered what he had heard about the LAPD's own OHS unit taking training in urban assault tactics. He wondered if Captain Hadley had a RAT team, too.

"They're going full field on this," Brenner said. "The Department of Homeland Security is overseeing from DC. This morning at nine there will be meetings on both coasts to bring everybody together on it."

"Who is everybody?"

"There's a protocol. We'll bring in Homeland, the JTTF, everybody. It'll be alphabet soup. The NRC, the DOE, RAP . . . who knows, before we get this contained we might even have FEMA setting up a tent. It's going to be federal pandemonium."

Bosch didn't know what all the acronyms stood for but didn't need to. They all spelled out *feds* to him.

"Who will be running the show?"

Brenner looked over at Bosch.

"Everybody and nobody. Like I said, pandemonium. If we open up that safe at Saint Aggy's and the cesium is gone, then our best shot at tracking it and getting it back will be to do it before all hell breaks loose at nine and we get micromanaged to death from Washington."

Bosch nodded. He thought maybe he had misjudged Brenner. The agent seemed to want to get things done, not wallow in the bureaucratic mire.

"And what's the LAPD status going to be in a full-field investigation?"

"I already told you, the LAPD remains in. Nothing changes on that. You remain in, Harry. My guess is that bridges are already being built between our people and your people. I know the LAPD has its own Homeland Security office. I am sure they will be brought in. We're obviously going to need all hands on deck with this."

Bosch glanced over at him. Brenner looked serious.

"Have you worked with our OHS before?" Bosch asked.

"On occasion. We shared some intelligence on a few things."

Bosch nodded but felt that Brenner was being disingenuous or was completely naive about the gulf between the locals and the feds. But he noted that he had been called by his first name and wondered if that was one of the bridges being built.

"You said you checked me out. Who did you check with?"

"Harry, we're working well here, why stir it up? If I made a mistake I apologize."

"Fine. Who'd you check me out with?"

"Look, all I'm going to tell you is that I asked Agent Walling who the LAPD point man was and she gave me your name. I made a few calls while driving in. I was told you were a very capable detective. That you had more than thirty years in, that a few years back you retired, didn't like it too much and came back to the job to work cold cases. Things went sideways in Echo Park—a little thing you dragged Agent Walling into. You were off the job a few months while that was, uh, cleared up and now you're back and assigned to Homicide Special."

"What else?"

"Harr—"

"What else?"

"Okay. The word I got is that you can be difficult to get along with—especially when it comes to working with the federal government. But I have to say, so far I don't see any of that at all."

Bosch figured that most of this information had come from Rachel—he remembered seeing her on the phone and her saying it was her partner. He was disappointed if she had said such things about him. And he knew that Brenner was probably holding back most of it. The truth was that he'd had so many run-ins with the feds—going back well before he ever met Rachel Walling—that they probably had a file on him as thick as a murder book.

After a minute or so of silence Bosch decided to change direction and spoke again.

"Tell me about cesium," he said.

"What did Agent Walling tell you?"

"Not much."

"It's a by-product. The fission of uranium and plutonium creates cesium. When Chernobyl hit meltdown, cesium was the stuff that was dispersed into the air. It comes in powder or a silver-gray metal. When they conducted nuke tests in the South Pacific—"

"I don't mean the science. I don't care about the science. Tell me about what we are dealing with here."

Brenner thought for a moment.

"Okay," he said. "The stuff we're talking about comes in pieces about the size of a pencil eraser. It is then contained in a sealed stainless steel tube about the size of a forty-five-caliber bullet cartridge. When used in the treatment of a gynecological cancer it is placed inside the woman's body—in the uterus—for a calculated amount of time and it irradiates the targeted area. It is supposed to be very effective in quick doses. And it is the job of a guy like Stanley Kent to make that calculus—to run the physics down and determine how long a dose is called for. He would then go and get the cesium out of the hospital's hot safe and deliver it in person to the oncologist in the operating room. The system is set up so that the doctor administering the treatment actually handles the stuff for as little time as possible. Because the surgeon can't wear any protection while performing a procedure, he's got to limit his exposure, you know what I mean?"

Bosch nodded.

"Do these tubes protect whoever handles them?"

"No, the only thing that knocks down the gamma rays from cesium is lead. The safe they keep the tubes in is lined with lead. The device they transport them in is made of lead."

"Okay. So how bad is this stuff going to be if it gets out there in the world?"

Brenner gave it some thought before answering.

"Out there in the world it is all about quantity, delivery and location," he said. "Those are the variables. Cesium has a thirty-year half-life. Generally, they consider ten half-lifes the safety margin."

"You're losing me. What's the bottom line?"

"The bottom line is that the radiation danger diminishes by half every thirty years. If you set off a good amount of this stuff in an enclosed environment—like maybe a subway station or an office building—then that place could be shut down for three hundred years."

Bosch was stunned as he registered this.

"What about people?" he asked.

"Also depends on dispersal and containment. A high-intensity exposure could kill you within a few hours. But if it's dispersed by an IED in a subway station, then my guess is the immediate casualties would be very low.

But a body count is not what this would be about. It's the fear factor that would be important to these people. You set something off like this domestically and what's important is the wave of fear it sends through the country. A place like Los Angeles? It would never be the same again."

Bosch just nodded. There was nothing else to say.

SIX

AT SAINT AGGY'S THEY ENTERED through the main lobby and asked the receptionist for the chief of security. They were told that the security chief worked days but that she would locate the night-shift security supervisor. While they waited they heard the helicopter land on the long front lawn of the medical center and soon the four-member radiological team came in, each man wearing a radiation suit and carrying a face guard. The leader of the group—it said KYLE REID on his nameplate—carried a handheld radiation monitor.

Finally after two prompts to the woman at

the front desk, a man who looked like he had been rousted from a bed in a spare patient room greeted them in the lobby. He said his name was Ed Romo and he couldn't seem to take his eyes off the hazmat suits worn by the members of the lab team. Brenner badged Romo and took charge. Bosch didn't object. He knew that they were now on turf where the federal agent would be best suited to walk point and maintain investigative velocity.

"We need to go to the hot lab and check the materials inventory," Brenner said. "We also need to see any records or key-card data that will show us who has been in and out of there in the last twenty-four hours."

Romo didn't move. He paused as if groping for understanding of the scene in front of him.

"What's this about?" he finally asked.

Brenner took a step closer to him and invaded his space.

"I just told you what it's about," he said. "We need to get into the hot lab in oncology. If you can't get us in there, then find somebody who can. Now."

"I gotta make a call first," Romo said.

"Good. Make it. I'll give you two minutes and then we're going to run you over."

The whole time he was making the threat Brenner was smiling and nodding.

Romo took out a cell phone and stepped away from the group to make the call. Brenner gave him the space. He looked at Bosch with a sardonic smile.

"Last year I did a security survey here. They had a key lock on the lab and the safe and that was it. They upgraded after that. But you build a better mousetrap and the mice just get smarter."

Bosch nodded.

Ten minutes later Bosch, Brenner, Romo and the rest of the lab team all stepped out of the elevator in the medical clinic's basement. Romo's boss was on his way in but Brenner was not waiting. Romo used a key card to gain entrance to the oncology lab.

The lab was deserted. Brenner found an inventory sheet and a lab log on an entrance desk and started reading. There was a small video monitor on the desk that showed a camera view of a safe.

"He was here," Brenner said.

"When?" Bosch asked.

"Seven o'clock, according to this."

Reid pointed to the monitor.

"Does that record?" he asked Romo. "Can

we see what Kent did when he was in there?"

Romo looked at the monitor as though it were the first time he had ever seen it.

"Um, no, it's just a monitor," he finally said. "Whoever's on the desk is supposed to watch whatever is taken out of the safe."

Romo pointed to the far end of the lab, where there was a large steel door. The trefoil warning symbol for radioactive materials was posted on it at eye level, along with a sign.

CAUTION!
RADIATION HAZARD

PROTECTIVE EQUIPMENT
MUST BE WORN

CUIDADO!
PELIGRO DE RADIACIÓN

SE DEBE USAR
EQUIPO DE PROTECCIÓN

Bosch noticed that the door had a push-button combination lock as well as a magnetic key-card swipe slot.

"It says here that he took one source of

cesium," Brenner said, as he continued to study the log. "One tube. It's a transfer case. He was taking the source over to Burbank Medical Center for a procedure there. It names the case. A patient named Hanover. It says that there were thirty-one pieces of cesium left in inventory."

"Is that all you need, then?" Romo asked.

"No," Brenner said. "We have to physically inspect the inventory. We'll need to enter the safe room and then open the safe. What's the combination?"

"I don't have it," Romo said.

"Who does?"

"The physicists. The head of the lab. The chief of security."

"And where is the chief of security?"

"I told you. He's coming."

"Get him on the speaker."

Brenner pointed to the phone on the desk. Romo sat down. He put the phone on speaker and tapped in a number from memory. It was answered immediately.

"This is Richard Romo."

Ed Romo leaned forward to the phone and looked as though he was embarrassed by the revelation of the obvious nepotism at play.

"Uh, yeah, Dad, this is Ed. The man from the FB—"

"Mr. Romo?" Brenner cut in. "This is Special Agent John Brenner of the FBI. I believe we met and spoke about security issues a year ago. How far away are you, sir?"

"Twenty to twenty-five minutes. I remember—"

"That's too far, sir. We need to open the hot lab safe right now to determine its contents."

"You can't open that without hospital approval. I don't care who—"

"Mr. Romo, we have reason to believe the contents of the safe were turned over to people without the interests or safety of the American people in mind. We need to open the safe so that we know exactly what is here and what is missing. And we can't wait twenty to twenty-five minutes to do it. Now, I have properly identified myself to your *son* and I have a radiation team in the lab right now. We have to *move,* sir. Now, how do we open the safe?"

There was silence from the speakerphone for a few moments. Then Richard Romo relented.

"Ed, I take it you are calling from the desk in the lab?"

"Yeah."

"Okay, unlock it and open the bottom-left drawer."

Ed Romo rolled his chair back and studied the desk. There was a key lock on the upper-left drawer that apparently unlocked all three drawers.

"Which key?" he asked.

"Hold on."

Over the speakerphone there was the sound of a key ring being jingled.

"Try fourteen-fourteen."

Ed Romo pulled a key ring off his belt and went through the keys until he found one stamped with the number 1414. He then inserted it into the lock on the desk drawer and turned it. The bottom drawer was now unlocked and he pulled it open.

"Got it."

"Okay, there's a binder in the drawer. Open it up and look for the page with the combination lists for the safe room. It's changed week to week."

Holding the binder in his hands, Romo started to open it at an angle that would allow only him to see the contents. Brenner reached across the desk and roughly took the binder from him. He opened it on the desk and started leafing through pages of safety protocols.

"Where is it?" he said impatiently to the speakerphone.

"It should be in the final section. It will be clearly marked as hot lab combinations. There is one catch, though. We use the previous week. The combination for the current week is wrong. Use last week's combo."

Brenner found the page and drew his finger down the listing until he found the combination for the previous week.

"Okay, got it. What about the safe inside?"

Richard Romo answered from his car.

"You will use the key card again and another combination. That one I know. It doesn't change. It is six-six-six."

"Original."

Brenner held his hand out to Ed Romo.

"Give me your key card."

Romo complied and Brenner then handed the card to Reid.

"Okay, Kyle, go," Brenner ordered. "The

door combo is five-six-one-eight-four and you heard the rest."

Reid turned and pointed to one of the others in hazmat suits.

"It'll be tight in there. Just Miller and I go in."

The leader and his chosen second snapped on their face guards and used the key card and combination to open the safe room door. Miller carried the radiation monitor and they entered the safe room, pulling the door closed behind them.

"You know, people go in there all the time and they don't wear space suits," Ed Romo said.

"I'm happy for them," Brenner said. "This situation is a little different, don't you think? We don't know what may or may not have been let loose in that environment."

"I was just saying," Romo said defensively.

"Then do me a favor and don't say anything, son. Let us do our job."

Bosch watched on the monitor and soon saw a glitch in the security system. The camera was mounted overhead, but as soon as Reid bent down to type the combination into the materials safe, he blocked the camera's view of what he was doing. Bosch knew that even if someone had watched Kent when he went into the safe at 7 p.m. the evening before, he could easily have hidden what he was taking.

Less than a minute after going into the safe room the two men in hazmat suits stepped out. Brenner stood up. The men unsnapped their face guards and Reid looked at Brenner. He shook his head.

"The safe's empty," he said.

Brenner pulled his phone from his pocket. But before he could punch in a number, Reid stepped forward, holding out a piece of paper torn from a spiral notebook.

"This was all that was left," he said.

Bosch looked over Brenner's shoulder at the note. It was scribbled in ink and difficult to decipher. Brenner read it out loud.

"'I am being watched. If I don't do this they'll kill my wife. Thirty-two sources, cesium. God forgive me. No choice.'"

SEVEN

BOSCH AND THE FEDERAL AGENTS stood silently. There was an almost palpable sense of dread hanging in the air in the oncology lab. They had just confirmed that Stanley Kent took thirty-two capsules of cesium from the safe at Saint Agatha's and then most likely turned them over to persons unknown. Those persons unknown had then executed him up on the Mulholland overlook.

"Thirty-two capsules of cesium," Bosch said. "How much damage could that do?"

Brenner looked at him somberly.

"We would have to ask the science people but my guess is that it could get the job done," he said. "If somebody out there wants to send a message, it would be heard loud and clear."

Bosch suddenly thought of something that didn't fit with the known set of facts.

"Wait a minute," he said. "Stanley Kent's radiation rings showed no exposure. How could he have taken all the cesium out of here and not lit up those warning devices like a Christmas tree?"

Brenner shook his head dismissively.

"He obviously used a pig."

"A what?"

"The pig is what they call the transfer device. It basically looks like a lead mop bucket on wheels. With a secured top, of course. It's heavy and built low to the ground—like a pig. So they call it a pig."

"And he could just waltz right in and out of here with something like that?"

Brenner pointed at the clipboard on the desk.

"Inter-hospital transfers of radioactive sources for cancer treatment are not unusual," he said. "He signed out one source but then took them all. That's what was unusual, but who was going to open up the pig and check?"

Bosch thought about the indentations he had seen in the floor of the Porsche's trunk. Something heavy had been carried in the car and was then removed. Now Bosch knew what it was and it was just one more indication of the worst-case scenario.

Bosch shook his head and Brenner thought it was because he was making a judgment about security in the lab.

"Let me tell you something," the agent said. "Before we came in last year and revamped their security, anybody wearing a doctor's white coat could have walked right in here and gotten whatever he wanted out of the safe. Security was nothing."

"I wasn't making a comment on security. I was—"

"I have to make a call," Brenner said.

He moved away from the others and pulled out his cell phone. Bosch decided to make his own call. He pulled out his phone, found a corner for privacy and called his partner.

"Ignacio, it's me. I'm just checking in."

"Call me Iggy, Harry. What's happening with you?"

"Nothing good. Kent emptied the safe. All the cesium is gone."

"Are you kidding me? That's the stuff you said could be used to make a dirty bomb?"

"That's the stuff and it looks like he turned over enough of it to do the job. Are you still at the scene?"

"Yeah, and listen, I've got a kid here who might've been a witness."

"What do you mean, 'might've' been a witness? Who is it, a neighbor?"

"No, it's sort of a screwy story. You know that house that was supposedly Madonna's?"

"Yeah."

"Yeah, well, she used to own it but doesn't anymore. I go up there to knock on the door and the guy who lives there now says he didn't see or hear anything—I'm getting the same thing at every door I knock on. So anyway, I'm leaving when I spot this guy hiding behind these big potted trees in the courtyard. I draw down on him and call backup, you know, thinking maybe he's our shooter from the overlook. But that's not what it is. Turns out it's a kid—twenty years old and just off the bus from Canada—and he thinks Madonna's still living in the house. He's got a star map that still lists her as living there and he's trying to see her or something—like a stalker. He climbed over a wall to get into the courtyard."

"Did he see the shooting?"

"He claims he didn't see or hear anything, but I don't know, Harry. I'm thinking he might've been stalking Madonna's place when the thing went down on the overlook. He then hides and tries to wait it out. Only I find him first."

Bosch was missing something in the story.

"Why would he hide? Why wouldn't he just get the hell out of there? We didn't find the body till three hours after the shooting."

"Yeah, I know. That part doesn't make sense. Maybe he was just scared or thought that if he was seen in the vicinity of the body he might get tagged as a suspect or some-thing."

Bosch nodded. It was a possibility.

"You holding him on the trespass?" he asked.

"Yeah. I talked to the guy who bought the place from Madonna and he'll work with us. He'll press charges if we need him to. So don't worry, we can hold him and work him with it."

"Good. Take him downtown, put him in a room and warm him up."

"You got it, Harry."

"And Ignacio, don't tell anybody about the cesium."

"Right. I won't."

Bosch closed the phone before Ferras could tell him to call him Iggy again. He listened to the end of Brenner's conversation. It was obvious that he wasn't talking to Walling. His manner and tone of voice was deferential. He was talking to a boss.

"According to the log here, seven o'clock," he said. "That puts the transfer at the overlook at around eight, so we're talking about a six-and-a-half-hour lead at this point."

Brenner listened some and then started to speak several times but was repeatedly cut off by the person on the other end of the line.

"Yes, sir," he finally said. "Yes, sir. We're on our way back in now."

He closed the phone and looked at Bosch.

"I'm going back in on the chopper. I have to lead a teleconference debriefing with Washington. I'd take you with me but I think you'd be better off on the ground, chasing the case. I'll have someone pick up my car later."

"No problem."

"Did your partner come up with a witness? Is that what I heard?"

Bosch had to wonder how Brenner had picked that up while conducting his own phone conversation.

"Maybe, but it sounds like a long shot. I'm going downtown to see about that right now."

Brenner nodded solemnly, then handed Bosch a business card.

"If you get anything, give me a call. All my information is on that. Anything at all, call."

Bosch took the card and put it in his pocket. He and the agents then left the lab and a few minutes later he watched the federal chopper take off into the black sky. He got in his car and pulled out of the clinic's parking lot to head south. Before hitting the freeway he gassed up at a station on San Fernando Road.

Traffic coming down into the center of the city was light and he cruised at a steady eighty. He turned the stereo on and picked a CD from the center console without looking at what it was. Five notes into the first song he knew it was a Japanese import from bassist Ron Carter. It was good driving music and he turned it up.

The music helped Bosch smooth out his thoughts. He realized the case was shifting. The feds, at least, were chasing the missing cesium instead of the killers. There was a subtle difference there that Bosch thought was important. He knew that he needed to keep his focus on the overlook and not lose sight at any time of the fact that this was a murder investigation.

"Find the killers, you find the cesium," he said out loud.

When he got downtown he took the Los Angeles Street exit and parked in the front lot at police headquarters. At this hour nobody would care that he wasn't a VIP or a member of command staff.

Parker Center was on its last legs. For nearly a decade a new police headquarters had been approved for construction but because of repeated budgetary and political delays the project had only inched toward realization. In the meantime, little had been done to keep the current headquarters from sliding into decrepitude. Now the new building was under way but it was an estimated four years from completion. Many who worked in Parker Center wondered if it could last that long.

The RHD squad room on the third floor was deserted when Bosch got there. He opened his cell phone and called his partner.

"Where are you?"

"Hey, Harry. I'm at SID. I'm getting what I can so I can start putting the murder book together. Are you in the office?"

"I just got here. Where'd you put the wit?"

"I've got him cooking in room two. You want to start with him?"

"Might be good to hit him with somebody he hasn't seen before. Somebody older."

It was a delicate suggestion. The potential witness was Ferras's find. Bosch wouldn't move in on him without his partner's at least tacit approval. But the situation dictated that someone with Bosch's experience would be better conducting such an important interview.

"Have at him, Harry. When I get back I'll watch in the media room. If you need me to come in, just give me the signal."

"Right."

"I made fresh coffee in the captain's office if you want it."

"Good. I need it. But first tell me about the witness."

"His name is Jesse Mitford. From Halifax. He's kind of a drifter. He told me he hitch-hiked down here and has been staying in shelters and sometimes up in the hills—when it's warm enough. That's about it."

It was pretty thin but it was a start.

"Maybe he was going to sleep up there in Madonna's courtyard. That's why he didn't split."

"I didn't think about that, Harry. You might be right."

"I'll be sure to ask him."

Bosch ended the call, got his coffee mug out of his desk drawer and headed to the RHD captain's office. There was an anteroom where the secretary's desk was located as well as a table with a coffeemaker. The smell of fresh-brewed coffee hit Bosch as he entered and that alone almost gave him the caffeine charge he needed. He poured a cup, dropped a buck in the basket and then headed back to his desk.

The squad room was designed with long rows of facing desks so that partners sat across from each other. The design afforded no personal or professional privacy. Most of the other detective bureaus in the city had gone to cubicles with sound and privacy walls but at Parker Center no money was spent on improvements because of the impending demolition.

Since Bosch and Ferras were the newest additions to the squad their desk tandem was located at the end of a line in a windowless corner where the air circulation was bad and they would be furthest from the exit in the case of an emergency like an earthquake.

Bosch's work space was neat and clean, just as he had left it. He noticed a backpack and a plastic evidence bag on his partner's desk across from him. He reached over and grabbed the backpack first. He opened it and found it contained mostly clothing and other personal items belonging to the potential witness. There was a book called *The Stand* by Stephen King and a bag with toothpaste and a toothbrush in it. It all amounted to the meager belongings of a meager existence.

He returned the backpack and reached across for the evidence bag next. It contained a small amount of U.S. currency, a set of keys, a thin wallet and a Canadian passport. It also contained a folded "Homes of the Stars" map that Bosch knew was the kind sold on street corners all around Hollywood. He unfolded it and located the overlook off Mulholland Drive above Lake Hollywood. Just to the left of the location there was a black star with the number 23 in it. It had been circled with an ink pen. He checked the map's index, and star number 23 said, *Madonna's Hollywood Home.*

The map had obviously not been updated with Madonna's movements and Bosch suspected that few of the star locations and their attendant celebrity listings were accurate. This explained why Jesse Mitford had been stalking a house where Madonna no longer lived.

Bosch refolded the map, put all the property back in the evidence bag and returned it to his partner's desk. He then got a legal pad and a rights waiver out of a drawer and stood up to go to interview room 2, which was located in a hallway off the back of the squad room.

Jesse Mitford looked younger than his years. He had curly, dark hair and ivory-white skin. He had a stubble of chin hair that looked like it might have taken him his whole life to grow. He had silver rings piercing one nostril and one eyebrow. He looked alert and scared. He was seated at a small table in the small interview room. The room smelled of body odor. Mitford was sweating, which of course was the object. Bosch had checked the thermostat in the hallway before coming in. Ferras had set the temperature in the interview room to eighty-two.

"Jesse, how are you doing?" Bosch asked as he took the empty seat across from him.

"Uh, not so good. It's hot in here."

"Really?"

"Are you my lawyer?"

"No, Jesse, I'm your detective. My name's Harry Bosch. I'm a homicide detective and I am working the overlook case."

Bosch put both his legal pad and his coffee mug down on the table. He noticed that Mitford still had handcuffs on. It was a nice touch by Ferras to keep the kid confused, scared and worried.

"I told the Mexican detective I didn't want to talk anymore. I want a lawyer."

Bosch nodded.

"He's Cuban American, Jesse," he said. "And you don't get a lawyer. Lawyers are for U.S. citizens only."

This was a lie but Bosch was banking on the twenty-year-old's not knowing this.

"You're in trouble, kid," he continued. "It's one thing to be stalking an old girlfriend or boyfriend. It's something else with a celebrity. This is a celebrity town in a celebrity country, Jesse, and we take care of our own. I don't know what you've got up there in Canada but the penalties here for what you were doing tonight are pretty stiff."

Mitford shook his head as if he could ward off his problems that way.

"But I was told that she doesn't even live there anymore. Madonna, I mean. So I wasn't really stalking her, then. It would just be trespassing."

Now Bosch shook his head.

"It's about intent, Jesse. You thought she might be there. You had a map that said she *was* there. You even circled the spot. So as far as the law goes, that constitutes stalking a celebrity."

"Then why do they sell maps to stars' homes?"

"And why do bars have parking lots when drunk driving is illegal? We're not going to play that game, Jesse. The point is, there's nothing on the map that says anything about

it being okay to jump over a wall and trespass, you know what I mean?"

Mitford dropped his eyes to his manacled
wrists and sadly nodded.

"Tell you what, though," Bosch said. "You
can cheer up because things aren't as bad
as they seem. You've got stalking and trespassing charges here, but I think we can
probably get this all fixed up and taken care
of if you agree to cooperate with me."

Mitford leaned forward.

"But like I told that Mexi—that Cuban detective, I didn't see anything."

Bosch waited a long moment before responding.

"I don't care what you told him. You're dealing with me now, son. And I think you're holding back on me."

"No, I'm not. I swear to God."

He held his hands open and as wide as
the cuffs allowed in a pleading gesture. But
Bosch wasn't buying it. The kid was too
young to be a liar capable of convincing
Bosch. He decided to go right at him.

"Let me tell you something, Jesse. My
partner is good and he's going places in the
department. No doubt about that. But right
now he's a baby. He's been a detective for

about as long as you've been growing that peach fuzz on your chin. Me, I've been around and that means I've been around a lot of liars. Sometimes I think all I know are liars. And, Jesse, I can tell. You're lying to me and nobody lies to me."

"No! I—"

"And so, what you've got here is about thirty seconds to start talking to me or I'm just going to take you down and book you into county lockup. I'm sure there's going to be somebody waiting in there who will have a guy like you singing *O Canada!* into the mike before sunup. You see, that's what I meant about there being stiff penalties for stalking."

Mitford stared down at his hands on the table. Bosch waited and twenty seconds slowly went by. Finally, Bosch stood up.

"Okay, Jesse, stand up. We're going."

"Wait, wait, wait!"

"For what? I said stand up! Let's go. This is a murder investigation and I'm not wasting time on—"

"All right, all right, I'll tell you. I saw the whole thing, okay? I saw everything."

Bosch studied him for a moment.

"You're talking about the overlook?" he

asked. "You saw the shooting on the over-look?"

"I saw everything, man."

Bosch pulled his chair out and sat back down.

EIGHT

BOSCH STOPPED JESSE MITFORD FROM SPEAKING until he signed a rights waiver. It didn't matter that he was now considered a witness to the murder that took place on the Mulholland overlook. Whatever it was that he witnessed he saw because he was in the act of committing his own crime—trespassing and stalking. Bosch had to make sure there were no mistakes on the case. No fruit-of-the-poison-tree appeal. No blowback. The stakes were high, the feds were classic second-guessers and he knew he had to do this right.

"Okay, Jesse," he said when the waiver form was signed. "You are going to tell me what you saw and heard up on the overlook. If you are truthful and helpful I am going to drop all charges and let you walk out of here a free man."

Technically, Bosch was overstating his hand. He had no authority to drop charges or make deals with criminal suspects. But he didn't need it in this case because Mitford had not yet been formally charged with anything. Therein lay Bosch's leverage. It came down to semantics. What Bosch was really offering was to not proceed with charging Mitford in exchange for the young Canadian's honest cooperation.

"I understand," Mitford said.

"Just remember, only the truth. Only what you saw and heard. Nothing else."

"I understand."

"Hold up your hands."

Mitford raised his wrists and Bosch used his own key to remove his partner's handcuffs. Mitford immediately began to rub them to get circulation going again. It reminded Bosch of seeing Rachel rub Alicia Kent's wrists earlier.

"Feel better?" he asked.

"Yeah, good," Mitford replied.

"Okay, then let's start from the top. Tell me

where you came from, where you were going and exactly what you saw up on the overlook."

Mitford nodded and then took Bosch through a twenty-minute story that began on Hollywood Boulevard with the purchase of the star map from a curbside vendor and his long trek on foot up into the hills. His journey took nearly three hours and probably accounted most for the odor emanating from his body. He told Bosch that by the time he got up to Mulholland Drive it was getting dark and he was tired. The house where the map said Madonna lived was dark inside. No one appeared to be home. Disappointed, he decided to rest from his long journey and to wait and see if the pop singer he wanted to meet would arrive home later. He found a spot behind some bushes where he could lean back against the exterior of the wall that surrounded the home of his quarry—he didn't use that word—and wait. Mitford said he fell asleep there until something woke him up.

"What woke you up?" Bosch asked.

"Voices. I heard voices."

"What was said?"

"I don't know. It was just what woke me up."

"How far were you from the overlook?"

"I don't know. Like fifty meters, I think. I was pretty far away."

"What was said after you were awake and could hear?"

"Nothing. They stopped."

"All right, then what did you see when you woke up?"

"I saw three cars parked by the clearing. One was a Porsche and the other two were bigger. I don't know the kind but they were sort of the same."

"Did you see the men on the overlook?"

"No, I didn't see anybody. It was too dark out there. But then I heard a voice again and it was coming from over there. In the dark. It was like a yell. Right at the moment I looked, there were two quick flashes and shots. Like muffled shots. I could see somebody in the clearing on his knees. You know, in the flash of light. But it was so quick that was all I saw."

Bosch nodded.

"This is good, Jesse. You're doing good. Let's just go over this part again so we have it right. You were asleep and then voices woke you up and you looked out and saw the three cars. Do I have that right?"

"Yes."

"Okay, good. Then you heard a voice again and you looked toward the overlook. Just then the shots were fired. Is all of that right?"

"Right."

Bosch nodded. But he knew that Mitford might be simply telling Bosch what he wanted to hear. He had to test the kid to make sure that wasn't happening.

"Now, you said that in the flash from the gun you saw the victim drop to his knees, is that right?"

"No, not exactly."

"Then tell me exactly what you saw."

"I think he was on his knees already. It was so fast I wouldn't have seen him drop to his knees like you said. I think he was already kneeling."

Bosch nodded. Mitford had passed the first test.

"Okay, good point. Now let's talk about what you heard. You said you heard somebody yell right before the shots, right?"

"Right."

"Okay, what did that person yell?"

The young man thought for a moment and then shook his head.

"I'm not sure."

"Okay, that's all right. We don't want to say anything we're not sure about. Let's try an exercise and see if that helps. Close your eyes."

"What?"

"Just close your eyes," Bosch said. "Think about what you saw. Try to bring up the visual memory and the audio will follow. You are looking at the three cars and then a voice pulls your attention toward the overlook. What did the voice say?"

Bosch spoke calmly and soothingly. Mitford followed his instructions and closed his eyes. Bosch waited.

"I'm not sure," the young man finally said. "I can't get it all. I think he was saying something about Allah and then he shot the guy."

Bosch held perfectly still for a moment before responding.

"Allah? You mean the Arabic word *Allah?*"

"I'm not sure. I think so."

"What else did you hear?"

"Nothing else. The shots cut it off, you know? He started yelling about Allah and then the shots drowned the rest out."

"You mean like *Allah Akbar,* is that what he yelled?"

"I don't know. I just heard the *Allah* part."

"Could you tell if he had an accent?"

"An accent? I couldn't tell. I only heard the one thing."

"British? Arabic?"

"I really couldn't tell. I was too far away and I only heard the one word."

Bosch thought about this for a few moments. He remembered what he had read about the cockpit recordings from the 9/11 attacks. The terrorists called out *Allah Akbar*—"God is greatest"—at the last moment. Did one of Stanley Kent's killers do the same?

Again, he knew he had to be careful and thorough. Much of the investigation could hinge on the one word Mitford thought he had heard from the overlook.

"Jesse, what did Detective Ferras tell you about this case before he put you in this room?"

The witness shrugged.

"He didn't tell me anything, really."

"He didn't tell you what we think we're looking at here or what direction the case may be going?"

"No, none of that."

Bosch looked at him for a few moments.

"Okay, Jesse," he finally said. "What happened next?"

"After the shots somebody ran from the
clearing to the cars. There was a streetlight
out there and I saw him. He got into one of
the cars and he backed it up close to the
Porsche. Then he popped the trunk and got
out. The Porsche's trunk was already open."

"Where was the other man while he did
this?"

Mitford looked confused.

"I guess he was dead."

"No, I mean the second bad guy. There
were two bad guys and one victim, Jesse.
Three cars, remember?"

Bosch held up three fingers as a visual
aid.

"I only saw one bad guy," Mitford said.
"The shooter. Somebody else stayed in the
car that was behind the Porsche. But he
never got out."

"He just stayed in that other car the whole
time?"

"That's right. In fact, right after the shooting, that car made a U-turn and drove away."

"And the driver never got out the whole
time he was at the overlook."

"Not while I was looking."

Bosch thought about this for a moment. What Mitford had described indicated a real division of labor between the two suspects. This mirrored the description of events that Alicia Kent had given earlier; one man questioning her and then translating and giving orders to the second. Bosch assumed it was the English speaker who had remained in the car at the overlook.

"Okay," he finally said, "go back to the story, Jesse. You said that right after the shooting one guy drives away while the other backs up closer to the Porsche and pops the trunk. Then what happened?"

"He got out and took something from the Porsche and put it in the other car's trunk. It was really heavy and he had a hard time with it. It looked like it had handles on the sides because of the way he was holding it."

Bosch knew that he was describing the pig used to transport radioactive materials.

"Then what?"

"He just got back in the car and drove off. He left the trunk open on the Porsche."

"And you saw nobody else?"

"Nobody else. I swear."

"Describe the man you did see."

"I can't really describe him. He was wearing a sweatshirt with the hood up. I never really saw his face or anything. I think that under the hood he was wearing a ski mask, too."

"Why do you think that?"

Mitford shrugged again.

"I don't know. It just seemed that way to me. I might be wrong."

"Was he big? Was he small?"

"I think he was average. Maybe a little short."

"What did he look like?"

Bosch had to try again. It was important. But Mitford shook his head.

"I couldn't see him," he insisted. "I'm pretty sure he had a mask."

Bosch didn't give up.

"White, black, Middle Eastern?"

"I couldn't tell. He had the hood and the mask and I was so far away."

"Think about the hands, Jesse. You said there were handles on the thing he transferred from one car to the other. Could you see his hands? What color were his hands?"

Mitford thought for a moment and his eyes brightened.

"No, he wore gloves. I remember the gloves because they were those real big kind like the guys wear who work on the trains back in Halifax. Heavy-duty with the big cuffs so they don't get burned."

Bosch nodded. He had been fishing for one thing but got something else. Protective gloves. He wondered if they were gloves specifically designed for handling radioactive material. He realized that he had forgotten to ask Alicia Kent if the men who entered her house had worn gloves. He hoped that Rachel Walling had covered all the details again when she was left with her.

Bosch paused there. Sometimes the silences are the most uneasy moments for a witness. They start to fill in the blanks.

But Mitford said nothing. After a long moment Bosch continued.

"Okay, we had two cars up there besides the Porsche. Describe the car that backed up to the Porsche."

"I can't, really. I know what Porsches look like, but I couldn't tell about the other cars. Both were a lot bigger, like with four doors."

"Let's talk about the one in front of the Porsche. Was it a sedan?"

"I don't know the brand."

"No, a sedan is a type of car, not a brand. Four doors, trunk—like a police car."

"Yes, like that."

Bosch thought about Alicia Kent's description of her missing car.

"Do you know what a Chrysler Three Hundred looks like?"

"No."

"What color was the car you saw?"

"I don't know for sure but it was dark. Black or dark blue."

"What about the other car? The one that was behind the Porsche."

"Same thing. A dark sedan. It was different from the one in front—maybe a little bit smaller, eh—but I don't know what kind it was. Sorry."

The boy frowned, as though it was a personal failing that he didn't know the makes and models of cars.

"It's all right, Jesse, you're doing fine," Bosch said. "You've been very helpful. Do you think if I showed you photos of various sedans you could pick out the cars?"

"No, I didn't see them enough. The lighting on the street wasn't good and I was too far away."

Bosch nodded but was disappointed. He considered things for a moment. Mitford's story matched up with information provided by Alicia Kent. The two intruders to the Kent house had to have had transportation to get there. One would have taken the original vehicle, while the other took Alicia Kent's Chrysler to transport the cesium with. It seemed like the obvious thing.

His thoughts prompted a new question for Mitford.

"Which way did the second car go when he drove off?"

"He also made a U-turn and drove down the hill."

"And that was it?"

"That was it."

"What did you do then?"

"Me? Nothing. I just stayed where I was."

"Why?"

"I was scared. I was pretty sure I had just seen some guy get murdered."

"You didn't go check on him to see if he was alive and needed help?"

Mitford looked away from Bosch and shook his head.

"No, I was afraid. I'm sorry."

"It's okay, Jesse. You don't have to worry about that. He was already dead. He was dead before he hit the ground. But what I'm curious about is why you stayed in hiding for so long. Why didn't you go down the hill? Why didn't you call nine-one-one?"

Mitford raised his hands and dropped them on the table.

"I don't know. I was afraid, I guess. I followed the map up the hill, so that was the only way I knew back. I would have had to walk right by there and I thought, what if the cops come while I'm walking right there? I could get blamed. And I thought, if it was like the mafia or something that did it and they found out I had seen everything, then I'd be killed or something."

Bosch nodded.

"I think you watch too much American TV up there in Canada. You don't have to worry. We'll take care of you. How old are you, Jesse?"

"Twenty."

"So, what were you doing at Madonna's house? Isn't she a little old for you?"

"No, it wasn't like that. It was for my mother."

"You were stalking her for your mother?"

"I'm not a stalker. I just wanted to get my mother her autograph or see if she had a picture or something I could have. I wanted to send something back to my mom and I don't have anything. You know, just to show her I'm okay. I thought if I told her I had met Madonna, then I wouldn't feel like such a . . . you know. I grew up listening to Madonna because my mom listens to her stuff. I just thought it would be kind of cool to send her something. Her birthday's coming up and I didn't have anything."

"Why'd you come to L.A., Jesse?"

"I don't know. It just seemed like the place to go. I was hoping I could get in a band or something. But it's looking like most people come here with their band already. I don't have one."

Bosch thought Mitford had adopted the pose of the wandering troubadour but there had been no guitar or other mobile instrument with his backpack in the squad room.

"Are you a musician or a singer?"

"I play the guitar but I had to pawn it a few days ago. I'll get it back."

"Where are you staying?"

"I don't really have a place right now. I was going to sleep up in the hills last night. I guess it's the real answer to why I didn't leave after I saw what happened to that guy up there. I really didn't have anyplace to go."

Bosch understood. Jesse Mitford was no

different from a thousand others who got off the bus every month or thumbed it into town. More dreams than plans or currency. More hope than cunning, skill or intelligence. Not all of those who fail to make it stalk those who do. But the one thing they all share is that desperate edge. And some never lose it, even after their names are put up in lights and they buy houses on top of the hills.

"Let's take a break here, Jesse," Bosch said. "I need to make a few phone calls and then we'll probably need to go over it all again. You cool with that? I'll also see about maybe getting you a hotel room or something."

Mitford nodded.

"Think about the cars and the guy you saw, Jesse. We need you to remember more details."

"I'm trying but I . . ."

He didn't finish and Bosch left him there.

In the hallway Bosch switched on the air conditioning in the interview room and set it at sixty-four. It would soon cool off in the room and instead of sweating, Mitford would start to get cold—though coming from Canada, maybe not. After he chilled for a while Bosch would take another run at him and see if anything new came out. He checked his watch. It was almost 5 a.m. and the case meeting the feds were organizing was not for another four hours. There was a lot to do but he still had some time to work with Mitford. The first round had been productive. There was no reason for him not to think there was more to be gained by a second go at it.

Out in the squad room Bosch found Ignacio Ferras working at his desk. He was turned in his seat and was typing on his laptop on a slide-out table. Bosch noticed that Mitford's property had been replaced on the desk by other evidence bags and file folders. It was everything from SID that the case had spawned so far on the two crime scenes.

"Harry, sorry I didn't get back in there to watch," Ferras said. "Anything new from the kid?"

"We're getting there. I'm just taking a break."

Ferras was thirty years old and had an athlete's body. On his desk was the trophy awarded him for being his academy class's top achiever in physical conditioning and testing. He was also handsome, with mocha skin and short-cropped hair. He had piercing green eyes.

Bosch stepped over to his own desk to use

the phone. He was going to wake up Lieutenant Gandle one more time to give him another update.

"You track the vic's gun yet?" he asked Ferras.

"Yeah, I got it off the ATF computer. He bought a twenty-two-caliber belly gun six months ago. Smith and Wesson."

Bosch nodded.

"A twenty-two fits," he said. "No exit wounds."

"Bullets check in but they don't check out."

Ferras delivered the line like a television commercial huckster and laughed at his own joke. Bosch thought about what was lying beneath the humor. Stanley Kent had been warned that his profession made him vulnerable. His response was to purchase a gun for protection.

And now Bosch was betting that the gun he'd bought had been used against him, had been used to kill him by a terrorist who called out the name of Allah as he pulled the trigger. What a world it was, Bosch thought, when someone could draw the courage to pull the trigger on another man by calling out to his God.

"Not a good way to go," Ferras said.

Bosch looked across the two desks at him.

"Let me tell you something," he said. "You know what you find out on this job?"

"No, what?"

"That there are no good ways to go."

NINE

BOSCH WENT TO THE CAPTAIN'S OFFICE to refill his coffee mug. When he reached into his pocket for another buck for the basket, he came out with Brenner's card and it reminded him of Brenner's request to be updated on the possibility of a witness. But Bosch had just finished updating Lieutenant Gandle on what the young Canadian said he had seen and heard at the overlook and together they had decided to keep Mitford under wraps for the time being. Until at least the 9 a.m. meeting, when it would be put-up or shut-up time with the feds. If the federal powers that be were going to keep the LAPD involved in the investigation, it would become clear at that meeting. Then it would be quid pro quo time. Bosch would share the witness's story in exchange for a share of the investigation.

Meantime, Gandle said he would send another update through the department's chain of command. With the latest revelation of the word *Allah* cropping up in the investigation, it was incumbent upon him to make sure the growing gravity of the case was communicated upward.

With his mug full he went back to his desk and started going through the evidence collected from the murder scene and the house where Alicia Kent had been held while her husband did the bidding of her captors.

He was already aware of most of what had been found at the murder scene. He started removing Stanley Kent's personal belongings from the evidence bags and examining them. At this stage they had been processed by Forensics and it was okay to handle them.

The first item was the physicist's Black-Berry. Bosch was not adept in a digital world and readily acknowledged this. He had mastered his own cell phone but it was a basic model that made and received calls, stored numbers in a directory, and did nothing else—as far as he knew. This meant that he was quite lost as he tried to manipulate the higher-evolution device.

"Harry, you need help with that?"

Bosch looked up and saw Ferras smiling at him. Bosch was embarrassed by his lack of technological skill but not to the point where he wouldn't accept help. That would turn his personal flaw into something worse.

"You know how to work this?"

"Sure."

"It has e-mail, right?"

"It should."

Bosch had to get up to hand the phone across both of their desks.

"About six o'clock yesterday Kent was sent an e-mail that was marked urgent from his wife. It had the photo in it of her tied up on their bed. I want you to find it and see if there is a way you can somehow print it out with the photo. I want to look at the photo again but bigger than on that little screen."

As Bosch had been speaking, Ferras had already been working the BlackBerry.

"No problem," he said. "What I can do is just forward the e-mail to my own e-mail account here. Then I'll open it up and print it out."

Ferras started using his thumbs to type on the phone's tiny keyboard. It looked like some sort of child's toy to Bosch. Like the ones he had seen kids use on planes. He didn't understand why people were always typing feverishly on their phones. He was sure it was some sort of warning, a sign of the decline of civilization or humanity but he couldn't put his finger on the right explanation for what he felt. The digital world was always billed as a great advancement but he remained skeptical.

"Okay, I found it and sent it," Ferras said. "It'll probably come through in a couple minutes and I will print it. What else?"

"Does that show what calls he made and what calls came in?"

Ferras didn't answer. He manipulated the controls on the phone.

"How far back do you want to go?" he asked.

"For now, how about going back till about noon yesterday," Bosch replied.

"Okay, I'm on the screen. You want me to show you how to use this thing or do you want me to just give you the numbers?"

Bosch got up and came around the row of

desks so he could look over his partner's shoulder at the phone's small screen.

"Just give me an overview for now and we'll run the whole picture down later," he said. "If you tried to teach me we'd be here forever."

Ferras nodded and smiled.

"Well," he said, "if he made or received a call to or from a number that was in his address book it is listed by the name associated with the number in the address book."

"Got it."

"It shows a lot of calls to and from the office and various hospitals and address book names—probably doctors he worked with— all through the afternoon. Three calls are marked 'Barry' and I am assuming that was his partner. I looked up the state corporate records online, and K and K Medical Physicists is owned by Kent and someone named Barry Kelber."

Bosch nodded.

"Yeah," he said, "that reminds me that we have to talk to the partner first thing this morning."

Bosch leaned across Ferras's desk to reach the notepad on his own desk. He then

wrote the name Barry Kelber down while Ferras was continuing to scroll through the cell
phone's call log.

"Now, here we are after six and he starts
alternately calling his home and his wife's
cell phone. I get the feeling that these
weren't answered because he's got ten calls
logged in three minutes. He was calling and
calling. And these were all made after he
received that urgent e-mail from his wife's
account."

Bosch saw the picture beginning to fill in a
little bit. Kent had a routine day on the job,
handled a lot of calls to and from people and
places familiar to him and then got the e-mail
from his wife's account. He saw the photo attached and started calling home. She didn't
answer, which only alarmed him further. Finally, he went out and did what the e-mail
instructed him to do. But for all his efforts and
following of orders, they still killed him on the
overlook.

"So, what went wrong?" he asked out
loud.

"What do you mean, Harry?"

"Up at the overlook. I still don't understand
why they killed him. He did what they wanted.
He turned over the stuff. What went wrong?"

"I don't know. Maybe they killed him because he saw one of their faces."

"The witness says the shooter was wearing a mask."

"Well, then maybe nothing went wrong. Maybe the plan was to kill him all along. They made that silencer, remember? And the way the guy yells out *Allah* doesn't make it sound like something went wrong. Makes it sound like part of a plan."

Bosch nodded.

"Then if that was the plan, why kill him and not her? Why leave a witness?"

"I don't know, Harry. But don't those hardcore Muslims have a rule about hurting women? Like it keeps them out of nirvana or heaven or whatever they call it?"

Bosch didn't answer the question because he didn't know about the cultural practices his partner had crudely referred to. But the question underlined for him how out of his element he was on the case. He was used to chasing killers motivated by greed or lust or any one of the big seven sins. Religious extremism wasn't often on the list.

Ferras put the BlackBerry down and turned back to his computer. Like many detectives he preferred to use his own laptop because the computers provided by the department were old and slow and most of them carried more viruses than a Hollywood Boulevard hooker.

He saved what he had been working on and opened up his e-mail screen. The e-mail forwarded from Kent's account was there. Ferras opened the e-mail and whistled when he saw the embedded photograph of Alicia Kent naked and tied up on the bed.

"Yeah, that would do it," he said.

Meaning that he understood why Kent had turned over the cesium. Ferras had been married for less than a year and had a baby on the way. Bosch was just starting to get to know his young partner but knew already that he was deeply in love with his wife. Under the glass top of his desk Ferras had a collage of photos of his bride. Under the glass on his side of the workstation Bosch had photos of murder victims whose killers he was still looking for.

"Make me a printout of that," Bosch said. "Blow it up if you can. And go ahead and keep playing with that phone. See what else you can find."

Bosch went back to his side of the workstation and sat down. Ferras enlarged and printed out the e-mail and photo on a color printer located at the back of the squad room. He went over and retrieved it and then brought it to Bosch.

Bosch already had his reading glasses on but from a desk drawer he pulled a rectangular magnifying glass he'd bought when he noticed that his prescription was no longer strong enough for the close-up work. He never used the magnifying glass when the squad room was crowded with detectives. He didn't want to give the others something to ridicule him with—either in jest or not.

He put the printout down on his desk and leaned over it with the magnifier. He first studied the bindings that held the woman's limbs behind her torso. The intruders had used six snap ties, placing one loop around each wrist and ankle, then one to link the ankles and the last one to link the wrist loops to the loop connecting the ankles.

It seemed like an overly complicated way to bind the woman's extremities. It was not the way Bosch would have done it if he were trying to quickly hog-tie a perhaps struggling woman. He would have used fewer bindings and made the work easier and quicker.

He wasn't sure what this meant or if it

meant anything at all. Perhaps Alicia Kent hadn't struggled at all and in return for her cooperation her captors used the extra links in order to make the time she was left bound on the bed less difficult. It seemed to Bosch that the way she had been bound meant that her arms and legs were not pulled behind her as far as they could have been.

Still, remembering the bruising on Alicia Kent's wrists, he realized that no matter what, the time she had spent hog-tied naked on the bed had not been easy. He decided that the only thing he knew for sure from studying the photo was that he needed to talk with Alicia Kent again and go over what had happened in more exacting detail.

On a fresh page of his notebook he wrote down his questions about the bindings. He planned to use the rest of the page to add more questions in preparation for an eventual follow-up interview with her.

Nothing else came to mind during his study of the photograph. When he was finished he put the magnifier aside and started skimming through the forensics reports from the murder scene. Nothing grabbed his attention there either and he quickly moved on to the reports and evidence from the Kent house.

Because he and Brenner had quickly left the house for Saint Agatha's, Bosch had not been there when the SID techs searched for evidence left behind by the intruders. He was anxious to see what, if anything, had been found.

But there was only one evidence bag and it contained the black plastic snap ties that had been used to bind Alicia Kent's wrists and ankles and that Rachel Walling had cut in order to free her.

"Wait a minute," Bosch said, holding up the clear plastic bag. "Is this the only evidence they bagged at the Kent house?"

Ferras looked up.

"It's the only bag they gave me. Did you check the evidence log? It should be in there. Maybe they're still processing some stuff."

Bosch looked through the documents Ferras had obtained until he found the forensic evidence log. Every item removed from a crime scene by the technicians was always entered on the log. It helped track the chain of evidence.

He found the log and noticed that it included several items removed by technicians from the Kent house, most of them tiny hair and fiber specimens. This was to be expected, though there was no telling if any of the specimens was related to the suspects. But in all his years working cases Bosch had yet to come across the immaculate crime scene. Plain and simple, it was a basic law of nature that when a crime takes place it always leaves its mark—no matter how small—on the environment. There is always a transfer. It is just a matter of finding it.

On the list each snap tie had been individually entered and these were followed by numerous hair and fiber specimens extracted from locations ranging from the master bedroom carpet to the sink trap in the guest bathroom. The mouse pad from the office computer was on the list as well as a Nikon camera's lens cap which had been found beneath the bed in the master bedroom. The last entry on the list was the most interesting to Bosch. The evidence was simply described as a cigarette ash.

Bosch could not think what value as evidence a cigarette ash could be.

"Is anybody still up there in SID from the Kent house search?" he asked Ferras.

"There was a half hour ago," Ferras answered. "Buzz Yates and the latents woman whose name I always forget."

Bosch picked up the phone and called the SID office.

"Scientific Investigation Division, Yates."

"Buzz, just the guy I wanted to talk to."

"Who's this?"

"Harry Bosch. On the search of the Kent house, tell me about this cigarette ash you collected."

"Oh, yeah, that was a cigarette that had burned down to just the ash. The FBI agent who was there asked me to collect it."

"Where was it?"

"She found it on top of the toilet tank in the guest bedroom. Like somebody had put their smoke down while they took a leak and then forgot about it. It burned all the way through and then out."

"So it was just ashes when she found it?"

"Right. A gray caterpillar. But she wanted us to collect it for her. She said their lab might be able to do something with—"

"Wait a minute, Buzz. You gave her the evidence?"

"Well, sort of. Yeah. She—"

"What do you mean 'sort of'? You either did or you didn't. Did you give Agent Walling the cigarette ashes you collected from my crime scene?"

"Yes," Yates conceded. "But not without a lot of discussion and assurances, Harry. She said the bureau's science lab could analyze the ashes and determine the type of tobacco, which would then allow them to determine country of origin. We can't do anything like that, Harry. We can't even touch that. She said it would be important to the investigation because they might be dealing with terrorists from outside the country. So I went along with it. She told me that once she worked an arson case where they found a single ash from the cigarette that lit the fire. They were able to tell what brand and that tied it to a specific suspect."

"And you believed her?"

"Well . . . yeah, I believed her."

"So you gave her my evidence."

Bosch said it in a resigned tone.

"Harry, it's not *your* evidence. We all work and play on the same team, don't we?"

"Yeah, Buzz, we do."

Bosch hung up the phone and cursed. Ferras asked him what was wrong but Bosch waved the question away.

"Just typical bureau bullshit."

"Harry, did you get any sleep at all before the call out?"

Bosch looked across the desks at his partner. He knew exactly where Ferras was
headed with that question.

"No," Bosch answered. "I was awake. But
lack of sleep has nothing to do with my frustration with the FBI. I've been doing this for
more years than you've been alive. I know
how to handle sleep deprivation."

He held his mug of coffee up.

"Cheers," he said.

"It's still not good, partner," Ferras responded. "Your ass is going to be dragging
in a while."

"Don't worry about me."

"Okay, Harry."

Bosch went back to thoughts about the
cigarette ash.

"What about photos?" he asked Ferras.
"Did you pick up photos from the Kent
house?"

"Yeah, they're here somewhere."

Ferras looked through the files on his
desk and came up with the folder containing the photos and passed it across. Bosch
looked through them and found three shots
from the guest bathroom. A full shot, an
angled shot of the toilet that showed the
line of ash on the tank lid, and a close-up of

the gray caterpillar, as Buzz Yates had called it.

He spread the three shots out and used his magnifier once again to study them. In the close-up shot of the ash the photographer had put a six-inch ruler down on the tank lid to give the shot scale. The ash was almost two inches long, almost a full cigarette.

"See anything yet, Sherlock?" Ferras asked.

Bosch looked up at him. His partner was smiling. Bosch didn't smile back, deciding that now he couldn't even use the magnifying glass in front of his own partner without getting ripped.

"Not yet, Watson," he said.

He thought that might keep Ferras quiet. Nobody wanted to be Watson.

He studied the shot of the toilet and noted the seat had been left up. The indication was that a male had used the bathroom to urinate. The cigarette ash would further indicate that it had been one of the two intruders'. Bosch looked at the wall above the toilet. There was a small framed photograph of a winter scene. The leafless trees and steel-gray sky made Bosch think of New York or somewhere else in the East.

The photo prompted Bosch to remember a case he had closed a year ago while he was still in the Open-Unsolved Unit. He picked up the phone and called SID again. When Yates answered, Bosch asked for the person who checked the Kent house for latent fingerprints.

"Hold on," Yates said.

Apparently still annoyed with Bosch from the earlier phone call, Yates took his time getting the latents tech to the phone. Bosch ended up holding for about four minutes, using his glass to go over the photos from the Kent house the whole time.

"This is Wittig," a voice finally said.

Bosch knew her from prior cases.

"Andrea, it's Harry Bosch. I want to ask you about the Kent house."

"What do you need?"

"Did you laser the guest bathroom?"

"Of course. Where they found the ash and the seat was up? Yes, I did that."

"Anything?"

"No, nothing. It was wiped."

"How about the wall up above the toilet?"

"Yes, I checked there, too. There was nothing."

"That's all I wanted to know. Thanks, Andrea."

"Have a good one."

Bosch hung up and looked at the photo of the ash. Something about it bugged him but he wasn't sure what.

"Harry, what were you asking about the wall over the toilet?"

Bosch looked at Ferras. Part of the reason the young detective was partnered with Bosch was so that the experienced detective could mentor the inexperienced detective. Bosch decided to put the Sherlock Holmes crack aside and tell him the story.

"About thirty years ago there was a case in Wilshire. This woman and her dog found drowned in her bathtub. The whole place had been wiped clean but the lid was left up on the toilet. That told them they were looking for a man. The toilet had been wiped but on the wall up behind it they found a palm print. The guy had taken a leak and leaned on the wall while doing it. By measuring the height of the palm they were able to figure out the guy's height. They also knew he was left-handed."

"How?"

"Because the print on the wall was a right palm. They figured a guy holds his tool with his preferred hand while taking a leak."

Ferras nodded in agreement.

"So they matched the palm to a suspect?"

"Yeah, but only after thirty years. We cleared it last year in Open-Unsolved. Not a lot of palms in the data banks back then. My partner and I came across the case and sent the palm through the box. We got a hit. We traced the guy to Ten Thousand Palms in the desert and went out there to get him. He pulled a gun and killed himself before we could make the arrest."

"Wow."

"Yeah. I always thought it was weird, you know?"

"What? Him killing himself?"

"No, not that. I thought it was kind of weird that we traced his palm to Ten Thousand Palms."

"Oh, yeah. Ironic. So you didn't get a chance to talk to him?"

"Not really. But we were sure it was him. And I sort of took his killing himself in front of us as an admission of guilt."

"No, yeah, of course. I just mean I would've

liked to talk to the guy and ask him why he killed the dog, that's all."

Bosch stared at his partner for a moment.

"I think if we had talked, we would have been more interested in why he killed the woman."

"Yeah, I know. I was just wondering, why the dog, you know?"

"I think he thought the dog might be able to identify him. Like the dog knew him and would react in his presence. He didn't want to risk it."

Ferras nodded like he accepted the explanation. Bosch had just made it up. The question about the dog had never come up during the investigation.

Ferras went back to his work, and Bosch leaned back in his chair and considered things about the case at hand. At the moment, it was a jumble of thoughts and questions. And once again most prominent in his mind was the basic question of why Stanley Kent was killed. Alicia Kent said the two men who held her captive had worn ski masks. Jesse Mitford said he thought the man he saw kill Kent on the overlook was wearing a ski mask. To Bosch this begged the questions why shoot Stanley Kent if he couldn't even identify you? and why wear the mask if the plan all along was to kill him? He supposed that wearing the mask could have been a ploy to falsely reassure Kent and to make him cooperative. But that conclusion didn't feel right to him either.

Once more he put the questions aside, deciding that he didn't have enough information yet to properly go at them. He drank some coffee and got ready to take another shot at Jesse Mitford in the interview room. But first he pulled out his phone. He still had Rachel Walling's number from the Echo Park case. He had decided never to delete it.

He pushed the button and called the number, preparing for it to have been disconnected by her. The number was still good but when he heard her voice it was a recording telling him to leave a message after the beep.

"It's Harry Bosch," he said. "I need to talk to you about things and I want my cigarette ashes back. That crime scene was mine."

He hung up. He knew the message would annoy her, maybe even make her mad. He knew that he was inextricably heading toward a confrontation with Rachel and the bureau that probably wasn't necessary and could easily be avoided.

But Bosch couldn't bring himself to roll over. Not even for Rachel and the memory of what they once had. Not even for the hope of a future with her that he still carried like a number in a cell phone's heart.

TEN

BOSCH AND FERRAS STEPPED OUT the front door of the Mark Twain Hotel and surveyed the morning. The light was just beginning to enter the sky. The marine layer was coming in gray and thick and was deepening the shadows in the streets. It made it look like a city of ghosts and that was fine with Bosch. It matched his outlook.

"You think he'll stay put?" Ferras asked.

Bosch shrugged.

"He's got no place else to go," he said.

They had just checked their witness into the hotel under the alias Stephen King. Jesse Mitford had turned into a valuable asset. He was Bosch's ace in the hole. Though he had not been able to provide a description of the man who shot Stanley Kent and took the cesium, Mitford had been able to give the investigators a clear understanding of what had transpired at the Mulholland overlook. He would also be useful if the investigation ever led to an arrest and trial. His story could be used as the narrative of the crime. A prosecutor could use him to connect the dots for the jury and that made him valuable, whether or not he could ID the shooter.

After Bosch had consulted with Lieutenant Gandle, it was decided that they shouldn't lose track of the young drifter. Gandle approved a hotel voucher that would keep Mitford in the Mark Twain for four days. By then things would be clearer in regard to which way the case was going to go.

Bosch and Ferras got into the Crown Victoria that Ferras had earlier checked out of the car shed and headed down Wilcox to Sunset. Bosch was behind the wheel. At the light he got out his cell phone. He hadn't heard back from Rachel Walling, so he called the number her partner had given him. Brenner answered right away and Bosch proceeded cautiously.

"Just checking in," he said. "We still on for the meeting at nine?"

Bosch wanted to make sure he was still part of the investigation before updating Brenner on anything.

"Uh, yes . . . yes, we're still on for the meeting but it's been pushed back."

"Till when?"

"I think it's ten now. We'll let you know."

The answer didn't make it sound like the meeting with the locals was a done deal. He decided to press Brenner.

"Where will it be? At Tactical?"

Bosch knew from working with Walling before that the Tactical unit was off campus in a secret location. He wanted to see if Brenner would slip.

"No, in the federal building downtown. Fourteenth floor. Just ask for the TIU meeting. How helpful was the witness?"

Bosch decided to hold his cards close until he had a better idea of his standing.

"He saw the shooting from a distance. Then he saw the transfer. He said one man did it all, killed Stanley Kent and then moved the pig from the Porsche to the back of another vehicle. The other guy waited in another car and just watched."

"You get any plates from him?"

"No, no plates. Mrs. Kent's car was probably the one used to make the transfer. That way there would be no cesium trace in their own car."

"What about the suspect he did see?"

"Like I said, he couldn't ID him. He was still wearing a ski mask. Other than that, nada."

There was a pause before Brenner responded.

"Too bad," he said. "What did you do with him?"

"The kid? We just dropped him off."

"Where's he live?"

"Halifax, Canada."

"Bosch, you know what I mean."

Bosch noticed the change in tone. That and the use of his last name. He didn't think Brenner was casually asking about Jesse Mitford's exact location.

"He's got no local address," he replied. "He's a drifter. We just dropped him off at the Denny's on Sunset. That's where he wanted to go. We gave him a twenty to cover breakfast."

Bosch felt Ferras staring at him as he lied.

"Can you hold a second, Harry?" Brenner said. "I've got another call coming in here. It might be Washington."

Back to first names, Bosch noted.

"Sure, Jack, but I can just go."

"No, hold on."

Bosch heard the line go to music and he looked over at Ferras. His partner started to speak.

"Why'd you tell him we—"

Bosch held a finger to his lips and Ferras stopped.

"Just hold it a second," Bosch said.

Half a minute went by while Bosch waited. A saxophone version of "What a Wonderful World" started to play on the phone. Bosch had always loved the line about the dark sacred night.

The light finally changed and Bosch turned onto Sunset. Then Brenner came back on the line.

"Harry? Sorry about that. That was Washington. As you can imagine, they're all over this thing."

Bosch decided to draw things out into the open.

"What's new on your end?"

"Not a lot. Homeland is sending a fleet of

choppers with equipment that can track a radiation trail. They'll start up at the overlook and try to pick up a signature specific to cesium. But the reality is it's got to come out of the pig before they'll pick up a signal. Meantime, we're organizing the status meeting so that we can make sure everybody's on the same page."

"That's all the big G has accomplished?"

"Well, we're just getting organized. I told you how it would be. Alphabet soup."

"Right. You called it pandemonium. The feds are good at that."

"No, I'm not sure I said all of that. But there's always a learning curve. I think after the meeting we'll be hitting this thing on all cylinders."

Bosch now knew for sure that things had changed. Brenner's defensive response told him the conversation was either being taped or overheard by others.

"It's still a few hours till the meeting," Brenner said. "What's your next move, Harry?"

Bosch hesitated but not for long.

"My next move is to go back up to the house and talk to Mrs. Kent again. I have some follow-up. Then we'll go over to the south tower at Cedars. Kent's office is there and we need to see it and to talk to his partner."

There was no response. Bosch was coming up on the Denny's on Sunset. He pulled into the lot and parked. Through the windows he could see that the twenty-four-hour restaurant was largely deserted.

"You still there, Jack?"

"Uh, yeah, Harry, I'm here. I should tell you that it probably won't be necessary, you going back to the house and then by Kent's office."

Bosch shook his head. *I knew it,* he thought.

"You've already scooped everybody up, haven't you?"

"Wasn't my call. Anyway, from what I hear, the office was clean and we have Kent's partner in here being questioned right now. We brought Mrs. Kent in as kind of a precautionary thing. We're still talking to her, too."

"Not your call? Then whose call was it, Rachel's?"

"I'm not going to get into that, Harry."

Bosch killed the car's engine and thought about how to respond.

"Well, then maybe my partner and I should

head downtown to TIU," he finally said. "This is still a homicide investigation. And last I heard, I was still working it."

There was a long thread of silence before Brenner responded.

"Look, Detective, the case is taking on larger dimensions. You have been invited to the status meeting. You and your partner. And at that time you will be updated on what Mr. Kelber has had to say and a few other things. If Mr. Kelber is still here with us I will do my best to get you in to speak with him. And with Mrs. Kent, too. But to be clear, the priority here is not the homicide. The priority is not finding out who killed Stanley Kent. The priority is finding the cesium and we're now almost ten hours behind."

Bosch nodded.

"I have a feeling that if you find the killer you find the cesium," he said.

"That may be so," Brenner responded. "But the experience is that this material is moved very quickly. Hand to hand. It takes an investigation with a lot of velocity. That's what we're engaged in now. Building velocity. We don't want to be slowed down."

"By the local yokels."

"You know what I mean."

"Sure. I'll see you at ten, Agent Brenner."

Bosch closed his phone and started to get out. As he and Ferras crossed the lot to the restaurant's doors, his partner barraged him with questions.

"Why did you lie to him about the wit, Harry? What's going on? What are we doing here?"

Bosch held his hands up in a calming motion.

"Hold on, Ignacio. Just hold on. Let's sit down and have some coffee and maybe something to eat and I'll tell you what is going on."

They almost had their pick of the place. Bosch went to a booth in a corner that would allow them a clear view of the front door. The waitress came over quickly. She was an old battle-ax with her steel-gray hair in a tight bun. Working graveyard at a Denny's in Hollywood had leached the life out of her eyes.

"Harry, it's been a long time," she said.

"Hey, Peggy. I guess it's been a while since I've had to chase a case through the night."

"Well, welcome back. What can I get you and your much younger partner?"

Bosch ignored the dig. He ordered coffee, toast and eggs-over medium well. Ferras ordered an egg-white omelet and a latte. When the waitress smirked and told him that neither could be accomplished he settled for scrambled eggs and regular coffee. As soon as the waitress left them alone Bosch answered Ferras's questions.

"We're being cut out," he said. "That's what's going on here."

"Are you sure? How do you know?"

"Because they've already scooped up our victim's wife and partner and I can guaran-damn-tee you they are not going to let us talk to them."

"Harry, did they say that? Did they tell you that we couldn't talk to them? There's a lot at stake here and I think you're being a little paranoid. You're jumping to—"

"Am I? Well, wait and see, partner. Watch and learn."

"We're still going to the meeting at nine, aren't we?"

"Supposedly. Except now it's at ten. And it will probably be a dog and pony show just for us. They're not going to tell us anything. They're going to sweet-talk us and brush us aside. 'Thanks a lot, fellas, we'll take it from here.' Well, fuck that. This is a homicide and nobody, not even the FBI, brushes me off a case."

"Have a little faith, Harry."

"I have faith in myself. That's it. I've been on this road before. I know where it goes. On the one hand, who cares? Let them run with the case. But on the other hand, I care. I can't trust them to do it right. They want the cesium. I want the bastards who terrorized Stanley Kent for two hours and then forced him down on his knees and put two slugs in the back of his head."

"This is national security, Harry. This is different. There's a greater good here. You know, the good of the order."

It sounded to Bosch like Ferras was quoting from an academy textbook or the code of some sort of secret society. He didn't care. He had his own code.

"The good of the order starts with that guy lying dead on the overlook. If we forget about him, then we can forget about everything else."

Nervous about debating his partner, Ferras had picked up the salt shaker and was manipulating it in his hand, spilling salt on the table.

"Nobody's forgetting, Harry. It's about priorities. I am sure that when things shake out during the meeting, they will share any information relating to the homicide."

Bosch grew frustrated. He was trying to teach the kid something but the kid wasn't listening.

"Let me tell you something about sharing with the feds," Bosch said. "When it comes to sharing information, the FBI eats like an elephant and shits like a mouse. I mean, don't you get it? There will be no meeting. They put that out there so we would stay in line until nine and now ten, all the while thinking we're still part of the team. But then we'll show up there and they'll delay it again and then they'll delay it again until they finally trot out with some organizational chart that's supposed to make us feel like we're part of everything when the reality is we're part of nothing and they've run out the back door."

Ferras nodded as though he was taking the advice to heart. But then he spoke from somewhere else.

"I still don't think we should have lied to them about the witness. He might be very valuable to them. Something he told us might fit with something they know about already.

What's the harm in telling them where he is? Maybe they take a shot at him and get something we didn't. Who knows?"

Bosch emphatically shook his head.

"No fucking way. Not yet. The wit is ours and we don't give him up. We trade him for access and information or we keep him for ourselves."

The waitress brought their plates and looked from the salt spilled on the table to Ferras and then Bosch.

"I know he's young, Harry, but can't you teach him some manners?"

"I'm trying, Peggy. But these young people don't want to learn."

"I hear you."

She left the table and Bosch immediately dug into his food, holding a fork in one hand and a piece of toast in the other. He was starved and had a feeling they'd be on the move soon. When they would next have time for a meal was anybody's guess.

He was halfway through his eggs when he saw four men in dark suits walk in with unmistakable federal purpose in their strides. Wordlessly, they split into twos and started walking through the restaurant.

There were less than a dozen diners in the

place, most of them strippers and their boyfriend pimps heading home from four o'clock
clubs, Hollywood night crawlers fueling the
engine before putting it to sleep. Bosch calmly
continued to eat and watched the men in
suits stop at each table, show credentials
and ask for IDs. Ferras was too busy splash-
ing hot sauce on his eggs to notice what was
happening. Bosch got his attention and nodded toward the agents.

Most of the people scattered among the
tables were too tired or buzzed to do anything but comply with the demands to show
identification. One young woman with a Z
shaved into the side of her head started giving one pair of agents some lip but she was a
woman and they were looking for a man, so
they ignored her and waited patiently for her
boyfriend with the matching Z to show some
ID.

Finally, a pair of agents came to the table
in the corner. Their creds identified them as
FBI agents Ronald Lundy and John Parkyn.
They ignored Bosch because he was too old
and asked Ferras for his ID.

"Who are you looking for?" Bosch asked.

"That's government business, sir. We just
need to check some IDs."

Ferras opened his badge wallet. On one side it had his photo and police ID and on the other side his detective's badge. It seemed to freeze the two agents.

"It's funny," Bosch said. "If you're looking at IDs that means you have a name. But I never gave Agent Brenner the witness's name. Makes me wonder. You guys over there in Tactical Intelligence don't happen to have a bug in our computer or maybe our squad room, do you?"

Lundy, the one obviously in charge of the pickup detail, looked squarely at Bosch. His eyes were as gray as gravel.

"And you are?" he asked.

"You want to see my ID, too? I haven't passed for a twenty-year-old in a long time, but I'll take it as a compliment."

He pulled out his badge wallet and handed it to Lundy unopened. The agent opened it and examined the contents very closely. He took his time.

"Hieronymus Bosch," he said, reading the name on the ID. "Wasn't there some sick creep of a painter named that? Or have I got it confused with one of the bottom-feeders I've read about in the overnights."

Bosch smiled back at him.

"Some people consider the painter a master of the Renaissance period," he said.

Lundy dropped the badge wallet on Bosch's plate. Bosch hadn't finished his eggs yet but luckily the yolks were overcooked.

"I don't know what the game is here, Bosch. Where's Jesse Mitford?"

Bosch picked up his badge wallet and used his napkin to clean egg debris off it. He took his time, put the wallet away and then he looked back up at Lundy.

"Who's Jesse Mitford?"

Lundy leaned down and put both hands on the table.

"You know damn well who he is and we need to take him in."

Bosch nodded as though he understood the situation perfectly.

"We can talk about Mitford and everything else at the meeting at ten. Right after I interview Kent's partner and his wife."

Lundy smiled in a way that carried no friendliness or humor.

"You know something, pal? You're going to need a Renaissance period yourself when this is all over."

Bosch smiled again.

"See you at the meeting, Agent Lundy. In

the meantime, we're eating. Can you go bother somebody else?"

Bosch picked up his knife and started spreading strawberry jam from a little plastic container on his last piece of toast.

Lundy straightened up and pointed at Bosch's chest.

"You better be careful, Bosch."

With that he turned and headed toward the door. He signaled to the other team of agents and pointed toward the exit. Bosch watched them go.

"Thanks for the heads-up," he said.

ELEVEN

THE SUN WAS STILL BELOW the ridgeline but dawn had a full grip on the sky. In daylight the Mulholland overlook showed no sign of the violence of the night before. Even the debris usually left behind at a crime scene—rubber gloves, coffee cups and yellow tape—had somehow been cleaned up or maybe had blown away. It was as if Stanley Kent had not been shot to death, his body never left on the promontory with the jetliner view of the city below. Bosch had investigated hundreds of murders during his time with the badge. He never got over how quickly the city seemed to heal itself—at least outwardly—and move on. To act as though nothing had ever happened.

Bosch kicked at the soft, orange ground and watched the dirt drop over the edge into the brush below. He made a decision and headed back toward the car. Ferras watched him go.

"What are you going to do?" Ferras asked.

"I'm going in. If you're coming, get in the car."

Ferras hesitated and then trotted after Bosch. They got back in the Crown Vic and drove over to Arrowhead Drive. Bosch knew that the feds had Alicia Kent but he still had the key ring from her husband's Porsche.

The fed car they had spotted when they had driven by ten minutes earlier was still parked in front of the Kent house. Bosch pulled into the driveway, got out and headed with purpose to the front door. He ignored the car in the street, even when he heard its door open. He managed to find the right key and get it into the lock before they were hit with a voice from behind.

"FBI. Hold it right there."

Bosch put his hand on the knob.

"Do not open that door."

Bosch turned and looked at the man approaching on the front walkway. He knew that whoever was assigned to watch the house would be the lowest man on the Tactical Intelligence totem pole, a screwup or an agent with baggage. He knew he could use this to his advantage.

"LAPD Homicide Special," he said. "We're just going to finish up in here."

"No, you're not," the agent said. "The bureau has taken over jurisdiction of this investigation and will be handling everything from here on out."

"Sorry, man, I didn't get the memo," Bosch said. "If you'll excuse us."

He turned back to the door.

"Do not open that door," the agent said again. "This is a national security investigation now. You can check with your superiors."

Bosch shook his head.

"You may have superiors. I have supervisors."

"Whatever. You're not going into that house."

"Harry," Ferras said. "Maybe we—"

Bosch waved a hand and cut him off. He turned back to the agent.

"Let me see some ID," he said.

The agent put an exasperated look on his face and dug out his creds. He flipped them open and held them out. Bosch was ready. He grabbed the agent by the wrist and pivoted. The agent's body came forward and past him and Bosch used a forearm to press him face first against the door. He pulled his hand—still clutching his credentials—behind his back.

The agent started struggling and protesting but it was too late. Bosch leaned his shoulder into him to keep him against the door and slipped his free hand under the man's jacket. He found and jerked the handcuffs off the agent's belt and started cuffing him up.

"Harry, what are you doing?" Ferras yelled.

"I told you. Nobody's pushing us aside."

Once he had the agent's hands cuffed behind him he grabbed the credentials out of his hand. He opened them and checked the name. Clifford Maxwell. Bosch turned him around and shoved the creds into the side pocket of his jacket.

"Your career is over," Maxwell said calmly.

"Tell me about it," Bosch said.

Maxwell looked at Ferras.

"You go along with this and you're in the toilet, too," he said. "You better think about it."

"Shut up, Cliff," Bosch said. "The only one who is going to be in the toilet is you when you go back to Tactical and tell them how you let two of the local yokels get the drop on you."

That shut him up. Bosch opened the front door and walked the agent in. He roughly pushed him down into a stuffed chair in the living room.

"Have a seat," he said. "And shut the fuck up."

He reached down and opened up Maxwell's jacket so he could see where he carried his weapon. His gun was in a pancake holster under his left arm. He would not be able to reach it with his wrists cuffed behind his back. Bosch frisked the agent's lower legs to make sure he wasn't carrying a throwdown. Satisfied, he stepped back.

"Relax now," he said. "We won't be long."

Bosch started down the hallway, signaling his partner to follow him.

"You start in the office and I'll start in the bedroom," he instructed. "We're looking for anything and everything. We'll know it when we see it. Check the computer. Anything unusual, I want to know about it."

"Harry."

Bosch stopped in the hallway and looked at Ferras. He could tell that his young partner was running scared. He let him have his say even though they were still within earshot of Maxwell.

"We shouldn't be doing it this way," Ferras said.

"How should we be doing it, Ignacio? Do you mean we should be going through channels? Have our boss talk to his boss, grab a latte and wait for permission to do our job?"

Ferras pointed down the hallway toward the living room.

"I understand the need for speed," he said. "But do you think he's going to let this go? He's going to have our badges, Harry, and I don't mind going down in the line of duty, but not for what we just did."

Bosch admired Ferras for saying *we* and that gave him the patience to calmly step back and put a hand on his partner's shoulder. He lowered his voice so Maxwell would not hear him from the living room.

"Listen to me, Ignacio, not one thing is going to happen to you because of this. Not one thing, okay? I've been around a little longer than you and I know how the bureau works. Hell, my ex-wife is ex-bureau, okay? And the one thing I know better than anything is that the number-one FBI priority is not to be embarrassed. That is a philosophy they teach them at Quantico and it seeps into the bones of every agent in every field office in every city. *Do not embarrass the bureau.* So when we are done here and we cut that guy loose he's not going to tell a single soul what we did or that we were even here. Why do you think they had him sitting on the house? Because he's F-B-Einstein? Uh-uh. He's working off an embarrassment—either to himself or the bureau. And he's not going to do or say a thing that brings him any more heat."

Bosch paused to allow Ferras to respond. He didn't.

"So let's just move quickly here and check out the house," Bosch continued. "When I was here this morning it was all about the widow and dealing with her and then we had to run out the door to Saint Aggy's. I want to take my time but be quick, you know what I mean? I want to see the place in daylight and grind the case down for a while. This is how I like to work. You'd be surprised what you come up with sometimes. The thing to re-member is that there's always a transfer. Those two killers left their mark somewhere in this house and I think SID and everybody else missed it. There's got to be a transfer. Let's go find it."

Ferras nodded.

"Okay, Harry."

Bosch clapped him on the shoulder.

"Good. I'll start in the bedroom. You check the office."

Bosch moved down the hallway and was to the threshold of the bedroom when Ferras called his name again. Bosch turned and went back down the hallway to the office al-cove. His partner was standing behind the desk.

"Where's the computer?" Ferras asked.

Bosch shook his head in frustration.

"It was on the desk. They took it."

"The FBI?"

"Who else? It wasn't on the SID log, only the mouse pad. Just look around, go through the desk. See what else you can find. We're not taking anything. We're just looking."

Bosch went down the hall to the master bedroom. It appeared to be undisturbed since he had last seen it. There was still a slight odor of urine due to the soiled mattress.

He walked over to the night table on the left side of the bed. He saw black fingerprint powder dusted across the knobs on the two drawers and its flat surfaces. On top of the table were a lamp and a framed photograph of Stanley and Alicia Kent. Bosch picked up the photo and studied it. The couple was standing next to a rosebush in full bloom. Alicia had dirt smudged on her face but was smiling broadly, as if she were standing proudly next to her own child. Bosch could tell that the rosebush was hers and in the background he could see others just like it. Farther up the hillside were the first three letters of the Hollywood sign and he realized the photo was probably taken in the backyard of the house. There would be no more pictures of the happy couple like this.

Bosch put the photo down and slid open the table's drawers one by one. They were full of personal items belonging to Stanley. Various reading glasses, books and prescription bottles. The lower drawer was empty and Bosch remembered that it was the place where Stanley had kept his gun.

Bosch closed the drawers and stepped

into the corner of the room on the other side of the table. He was looking for a new angle, some sort of fresh take on the crime scene. He realized that he needed the crime scene photos and he had left them in a file in the car.

He walked down the hallway toward the front door. When he got to the living room he saw Maxwell lying on the floor in front of the chair he had been placed in. He had managed to move his handcuffed wrists down over his hips. His knees were bent up with his wrists cuffed behind them. He looked up at Bosch with a red and sweating face.

"I'm stuck," Maxwell said. "Help me out."

Bosch almost laughed.

"In a minute."

He walked out the front door and went to the car, where he retrieved the files containing the SID crime scene reports and photos. He had put the copy of the e-mailed photo of Alicia Kent in there as well.

As he walked back into the house and headed toward the hallway to the rear rooms, Maxwell called out to him.

"Come on, help me out, man."

Bosch ignored him. He walked down the hallway and glanced into the home office as he passed. Ferras was going through the drawers of the desk, stacking things he wanted to look at on top of it.

In the bedroom Bosch got the e-mail photo out and put the files down on the bed. He held the photo up so he could compare it to the room. He then went to the mirrored closet door and opened it at an angle that matched the photograph. He noticed in the photo the white terry-cloth robe draped over a lounge chair in the corner of the room. He stepped into the closet and looked for the robe, found it and put it in the same position on the lounge chair.

Bosch moved to the place in the room from which he believed the e-mail photo had been taken. He scanned the room, hoping something would poke through and speak to him. He noticed the dead clock on the bed table and then checked it against the e-mail photo. The clock was dead in the photo, too.

Bosch walked over to the table, crouched and looked behind it. The clock was unplugged. He reached behind the table and plugged it back in. The digital screen started flashing 12:00 in red numerals. The clock worked. It just needed to be set.

Bosch thought about this and knew it

would be something to ask Alicia Kent about. He assumed the men who were in the house had unplugged the clock. The question was why. Perhaps they didn't want Alicia Kent to know how much or how little time had gone by while she waited tied up on the bed.

Bosch put the clock issue aside and moved to the bed, where he opened one of the files and took out the crime scene photographs. He studied these and noticed that the closet door was open at a slightly different angle from the one in the e-mail photo and that the robe was gone, obviously because Alicia Kent had put it on after her rescue. He stepped over to the closet, matched the door's angle to the one in the crime scene photograph, and then stepped back to the door and scanned the room.

Nothing broke through. The transfer still eluded him. He felt discomfort in his gut. He felt as though he was missing something. Something that was right there in the room with him.

Failure brings pressure. Bosch checked his watch and saw that the federal meeting—if there was actually going to be one—was to begin in less than three hours.

He left the bedroom and made his way

down the hall toward the kitchen, stopping in each room and checking closets and drawers and finding nothing suspicious or amiss. In the workout room he opened a closet door and found it lined with musty cold-weather clothes on hangers. The Kents had obviously migrated to L.A. from colder climes. And like most people who came from somewhere else, they refused to part with their winter gear. Nobody ever knew for sure how much of L.A. they could take. It was always good to be ready to run.

He left the contents of the closet untouched and closed the door. Before leaving the room he noticed a rectangular discoloration on the wall next to the hooks where rubber workout mats hung. There were slight tape marks indicating that a poster or maybe a large calendar had been taped to the wall.

When he got to the living room Maxwell was still on the floor, red-faced and sweating from struggling. He now had one leg through the loop created by his cuffed wrists, but he apparently couldn't get the other through in order to bring his hands to the front of his body. He was lying on the tiled floor with his wrists bound between his legs. He reminded

Bosch of a five-year-old holding himself in an effort to maintain bladder control.

"We're almost out of here, Agent Maxwell," Bosch said.

Maxwell didn't respond.

In the kitchen Bosch went to the back door and stepped out onto a rear patio and garden. Seeing the yard in daylight changed his perspective. It was on an incline and he counted four rows of rosebushes going up the embankment. Some were in bloom and some weren't. Some relied on support sticks that carried markers identifying the different kinds of roses. He stepped up the hillside and studied a few of these, then returned to the house.

After locking the door behind him, he walked across the kitchen and opened another door, which he knew led to the adjoining two-car garage. A bank of cabinets stretched along the back wall of the garage. One by one he opened them and surveyed the contents. There were mostly tools for gardening and household chores, and several bags of fertilizer and soil nutrients for growing roses.

There was a wheeled trash can in the garage. Bosch opened it and saw one plastic trash bag in it. He pulled it out, loosened the pull strap and discovered it contained what appeared to be only basic kitchen trash. On top was a cluster of paper towels that were stained purple. It looked like someone had cleaned up a spill. He held one of the towels up and smelled grape juice on it.

After returning the trash to the container Bosch left the garage and ran into his partner in the kitchen.

"He's trying to get loose," Ferras said of Maxwell.

"Let him try. Are you finished in the office?"

"Just about. I was wondering where you were."

"Go finish up and we'll be out of here."

After Ferras was gone Bosch checked the kitchen cabinets and the walk-in pantry and studied all the groceries and supplies stacked on the shelves. After that he went to the guest bathroom in the hall and looked at the spot where the cigarette ash had been collected. On the white porcelain tank top there was a brown discoloration about half the length of a cigarette.

Bosch stared at the mark, curious. It had

been seven years since he had smoked but he didn't remember ever leaving a cigarette to burn like that. If he had finished it he would have thrown it into the toilet and flushed it away. It was clear that this cigarette had been forgotten.

With his search complete, he stepped back into the living room and called to his partner.

"Ignacio, you ready? We're leaving."

Maxwell was still on the floor but looked tired from his struggle and resigned to his predicament.

"Come on, damn it!" he finally cried out. "Uncuff me!"

Bosch stepped close to him.

"Where's your key?" he asked.

"Coat pocket. Left side."

Bosch bent over and worked his hand into the agent's coat pocket. He pulled out a set of keys and fingered through them until he found the cuff key. He grabbed the chain between the two cuffs and pulled up so he could work the key in. He wasn't gentle about it.

"Now be nice if I do this," he said.

"Nice? I'm going to kick your fucking ass."

Bosch let go of the chain and Maxwell's wrists dropped to the floor.

"What are you doing?" Maxwell yelled. "Undo me!"

"Here's a tip, Cliff. Next time you threaten to kick my ass, you might want to wait until after I've cut you loose."

Bosch straightened up and tossed the keys onto the floor on the other side of the room.

"Uncuff yourself."

Bosch headed to the front door. Ferras was already going through it. As Bosch was pulling it closed he looked back at Maxwell sprawled on the floor. The agent's face was as red as a stop sign as he sputtered one last threat in Bosch's direction.

"This isn't over, asshole."

"Got it."

Bosch closed the door. When he got to the car he looked over the roof at his partner. Ferras looked as mortified as some of the suspects who had ridden in the backseat.

"Cheer up," Bosch said.

As he got in he had a vision of the FBI agent crawling in his nice suit across the living room floor to the keys.

Bosch smiled.

TWELVE

On the way back down the hill to the freeway Ferras was silent and Bosch knew he had to be thinking about the jeopardy his young and promising career had been placed in because of his old and reckless partner's actions. Bosch tried to draw him out of it.

"Well, that was a bust," he said. "I got nada. You find anything in the office?"

"Nothing much. I showed you, the computer was gone."

There was a sullen tone in his voice.

"What about the desk?" Bosch asked.

"It was mostly empty. One drawer had tax returns and stuff like that. Another had a copy

of a trust. Their house, an investment property in Laguna, insurance policies, everything
like that is held in a trust. Their passports
were in the desk, too."

"Got it. How much the guy make last
year?"

"A quarter million take-home. He also owns
fifty-one percent of the company."

"The wife make anything?"

"No income. Doesn't work."

Bosch grew quiet as he contemplated
things. When they got down off the mountain
he decided not to get on the freeway. Instead
he took Cahuenga to Franklin and turned
east. Ferras was looking out the passenger-
side window but quickly noticed the detour.

"What's going on? I thought we were going downtown."

"We're going to Los Feliz first."

"What's in Los Feliz?"

"The Donut Hole on Vermont."

"We just ate an hour ago."

Bosch checked his watch. It was almost
eight and he hoped he wasn't too late.

"I'm not going for the doughnuts."

Ferras cursed and shook his head.

"You're going to talk to the Man?" he asked.
"Are you kidding?"

"Unless I missed him already. If you're worried about it you can stay in the car."

"You're jumping about five links in the chain, you know. Lieutenant Gandle is going to have our asses for this."

"He'll have *my* ass. You stay in the car. It will be like you weren't even there."

"Except what one partner does, the other always gets equal blame for. You know that. That's how it works. That's why they call them *partners,* Harry."

"Look, I'll take care of it. There's no time to go through proper channels. The chief should know what is what and I'm going to tell him. He'll probably end up thanking us for the heads-up."

"Yeah, well, Lieutenant Gandle won't be thanking us."

"Then I'll deal with him, too."

The partners drove the rest of the way in silence.

The Los Angeles Police Department was one of the most insular bureaucracies in the world. It had survived for more than a century by rarely looking outward for ideas, answers or leaders. A few years earlier, when the city council decided that after years of scandal and community upset it required leadership from outside the department, it was only the second time in the LAPD's long history that the position of chief of police was not filled by promoting from within the ranks. Subsequently, the outsider who was brought in to run the show was viewed with tremendous curiosity, not to mention skepticism. His movements and habits were documented and the data was all dumped into an informal police pipeline that connected the department's ten thousand officers like the blood vessels in a closed fist. The intelligence was passed around in roll calls and locker rooms, text messages to and from patrol car computers, e-mails and phone calls, at cop bars and backyard barbecues. It meant street officers in South L.A. knew what Hollywood premiere the new chief had attended the night before. Vice officers in the Valley knew where he took his dress uniforms to be pressed and the gang detail in Venice knew what supermarket his wife liked to shop at.

It also meant that Detective Harry Bosch and his partner Ignacio Ferras knew what doughnut shop the chief stopped at for coffee every morning on his way into Parker Center.

At 8 a.m. Bosch pulled into the parking lot

of the Donut Hole but saw no sign of the chief's unmarked car. The business was an aptly named establishment in the flats below the hillside neighborhoods of Los Feliz. Bosch killed the engine and looked over at his partner.

"You staying?"

Ferras was looking straight ahead through the windshield. He nodded without looking at Bosch.

"Suit yourself," Bosch said.

"Listen, Harry, no offense but this isn't working. You don't want a partner. You want a gofer and somebody who doesn't question anything you do. I think I'm going to talk to the lieutenant about hooking me up with someone else."

Bosch looked at him and composed his thoughts.

"Ignacio, it's our first case together. Don't you think you should give it some time? That's all Gandle's going to tell you. He's going to tell you that you don't want to start out in RHD with a reputation as a guy who cuts and runs on his partner."

"I'm not cutting and running. It's just not working right."

"Ignacio, you're making a mistake."

"No, I think it would be best. For both of us."

Bosch stared at him for a long moment before turning to the door.

"Like I said, suit yourself."

Bosch got out and headed toward the doughnut shop. He was disappointed in Ferras's reaction and decisions but knew he should cut him some slack. The guy had a kid on the way and needed to play it safe. Bosch was not one to ever play it safe and it had lost him more than a partner in the past. He would take another shot at changing the young man's mind once the case settled down.

Inside the shop Bosch waited in line behind two people and then ordered a black coffee from the Asian man behind the counter.

"No doughnut?"

"No, just coffee."

"Cappuccino?"

"No, black coffee."

Disappointed with the meager sale, the man turned to a brewer on the back wall and filled a cup. When he turned back around, Bosch had his badge out.

"Has the chief been in yet?"

The man hesitated. He had no idea about the intelligence pipeline and was unsure about responding. He knew he could lose a high-profile customer if he spoke out of turn.

"It's all right," Bosch said. "I'm supposed to meet him here. I'm late."

Bosch tried to smile as though he was in trouble. It didn't come out right and he stopped.

"He not here yet," the counterman said.

Relieved he hadn't missed him, Bosch paid for the coffee and put the change in the tip jar. He went to an empty table in the corner. It was mostly a takeout operation at this time of morning. People grabbing fuel on their way into work. For ten minutes Bosch watched a cross section of the city's culture step up to the counter, all united by the addiction to caffeine and sugar.

Finally, he saw the black Town Car pull in. The chief was riding in the front passenger seat. Both he and the driver got out. Both scanned their surroundings and headed toward the doughnut shop. Bosch knew the driver was an officer and served as a bodyguard as well.

There was no line at the counter when they came in.

"Hiyou, Chief," the counterman said.

"Good morning, Mr. Ming," the chief responded. "I'll have the usual."

Bosch stood up and approached. The bodyguard, who was standing behind the chief, turned and squared himself in Bosch's direction. Bosch stopped.

"Chief, can I buy you a cup of coffee?" Bosch asked.

The chief turned and did a double take when he recognized Bosch and realized he wasn't a citizen wanting to make nice. For a moment Bosch saw a frown move across the man's face—he was still dealing with some of the fallout from the Echo Park case—but then it quickly disappeared into impassivity.

"Detective Bosch," he said. "You're not here to give me bad news, are you?"

"More like a heads-up, sir."

The chief turned away to accept a cup of coffee and a small bag from Ming.

"Have a seat," he said. "I have about five minutes and I'll pay for my own coffee."

Bosch went back to the same table as the chief paid for his coffee and doughnuts. He sat down and waited while the chief took his purchase to another counter and put cream and sweetener into his coffee. Bosch believed that the chief had been good for the department. He had made a few missteps politically and some questionable choices in command staff assignments but had largely been responsible for raising the morale of the rank and file.

That was no easy task. The chief had inherited a department operating under a federal consent decree negotiated in the wake of the FBI's Rampart corruption probe and myriad other scandals. All aspects of operation and performance were subject to review and compliance assessment by federal monitors. The result was that the department was not only answering to the feds but was awash in federal paperwork. Already an undersized department, it was hard sometimes to see where any police work was getting done. But under the new chief the rank and file had somehow pulled together to get the job done. Crime stats were even down, which to Bosch meant there was a good possibility that actual crime was down as well—he viewed crime statistics with suspicion.

But all of that aside, Bosch liked the chief for one overarching reason. Two years earlier he had given Bosch his job back. Bosch had retired and gone private. It didn't take him long to realize it was a mistake and when he did, the new chief welcomed him back. It made Bosch loyal and that was one reason he was forcing the meeting at the doughnut shop.

The chief sat down across from him.

"You're lucky, Detective. Most days I would have been here and gone an hour ago. But I worked late last night hitting Crime Watch meetings in three parts of the city."

Rather than open his doughnut bag and reach in, the chief tore it down the middle so he could spread it and eat his two dough-nuts off it. He had a powdered-sugar and a chocolate-glazed.

"Here's the most dangerous killer in the city," he said as he raised the chocolate-glazed doughnut and took a bite.

Bosch nodded.

"You're probably right."

Bosch smiled uneasily and tried an ice-breaker. His old partner Kiz Rider had just come back to work after recovering from gun-shot wounds. She transferred out of Rob-bery-Homicide to the chief's office, where she had worked once before.

"How's my old partner doing, Chief?"

"Kiz? Kiz is good. She does fine work for me and I think she's in the right spot."

Bosch nodded again. He did that a lot.

"Are you in the right spot, Detective?"

Bosch looked at the chief and wondered if he might already be questioning his jumping the chain of command. Before he could work up an answer the chief asked another question.

"Are you here about the Mulholland overlook case?"

Bosch nodded. He assumed that the word had gone up the pipe from Lieutenant Gandle and that the chief had been briefed in some detail about the case.

"I work out for an hour every morning just so I can eat this stuff," the chief said. "The overnights are faxed to me and I read them on the recumbent bike. I know you caught the overlook case and it's got federal interest. Captain Hadley also called me this morning. He said there is a terrorism angle."

Bosch was surprised to learn that Captain Done Badly and the OHS were already in the picture.

"What is Captain Hadley doing?" he asked. "He hasn't called me."

"The usual. Checking our own intelligence, trying to open lines with the feds."

Bosch nodded.

"So, what can you tell me, Detective? Why did you come here?"

Bosch gave him a fuller rundown on the case, accenting the federal involvement and what was looking like an effort to shut the LAPD out of its own investigation. Bosch acknowledged that the missing cesium was a priority and true cause for the feds to throw their weight around. But he said the case was a homicide, and that cut the LAPD in. He went over the evidence he had collected and laid out some of the theories he had been considering.

The chief had consumed both doughnuts by the time Bosch was finished. He wiped his mouth with a napkin and then checked his watch before responding. They were well past the five minutes he had initially offered.

"What aren't you telling me?" he asked.

Bosch shrugged.

"Not much. I just had a little dustup with an agent at the victim's house but I don't think anything will come of it."

"Why isn't your partner in here? Why is he waiting in the car?"

Bosch understood. The chief had seen Ferras when he scanned the lot upon his arrival.

"We're having a little bit of a disagreement on how to proceed. He's a good kid but he wants to roll over for the feds a little too easy."

"And of course we don't do that in the LAPD."

"Not in my time, Chief."

"Did your partner think it was appropriate to ignore the department's chain of command by coming directly to me with this?"

Bosch dropped his eyes to the table. The chief's voice had taken on a stern tone.

"As a matter of fact he wasn't happy about it, Chief," Bosch said. "It wasn't his idea. It was mine. I just didn't think there was enough time to—"

"Doesn't matter what you thought. It's what you did. So if I were you I would keep this meeting to yourself and I will as well. Don't ever do it this way again, Detective. Are we clear on that?"

"Yes, clear."

The chief glanced toward the glass display case where the doughnuts were lined up on trays.

"And by the way, how did you know that I would be here?" he asked.

Bosch shrugged.

"I don't remember. I just sort of knew."

He then realized that the chief might be thinking that Bosch's source was his old partner.

"It wasn't Kiz, if that's what you mean, Chief," he said quickly. "It's just something that gets known, you know? Word gets around the department."

The police chief nodded.

"It's too bad," he said. "I liked this place. Convenient, good doughnuts and Mr. Ming takes care of me. What a shame."

Bosch realized that the chief would now have to change his routine. It did not serve him well if it was known where he could be found and when.

"Sorry, sir," Bosch said. "But if I might make a recommendation. There's a place in the Farmer's Market called Bob's Coffee and Doughnuts. It's a bit out of the way for you but the coffee and doughnuts would be worth it."

The chief nodded thoughtfully.

"I'll keep it in mind. Now, what is it you want from me, Detective Bosch?"

Bosch decided that the chief obviously wanted to get down to business.

"I need to take the case where it goes and to do that I need access to Alicia Kent and her husband's partner, a guy named Kelber. The feds have them both and I think my window of access closed about five hours ago."

After a pause, Bosch got to the point of the whole unscheduled meeting.

"That's why I'm here, Chief. I need access. I figure you can get it for me."

The chief nodded.

"Besides my position in the department, I sit on the Joint-Terrorism Task Force. I can make some calls, raise some hell and probably open the window. As I said before, we have Captain Hadley's unit on this already and perhaps he can open up the channels of communication. We have been kept out of the loop on these things in the past. I can raise the flag, put in a call to the director."

To Bosch it sounded like the chief was going to go to bat for him.

"You know what reflux is, Detective?"

"Reflux?"

"It's a condition where all the bile backs up into your throat. It burns, Detective."

"Oh."

"What I am telling you is that if I make these moves and I get that window open for you, I don't want any reflux. You understand me?"

"I understand."

The chief wiped his mouth again and put the napkin down on his torn bag. He then crumpled it all into a ball, careful not to spill any powdered sugar on his black suit.

"I'll make the calls but it's going to be tough. You don't see the political angle here, do you, Bosch?"

Bosch looked at him.

"Sir?"

"The bigger picture, Detective. You see this as a homicide investigation. It is actually much more than that. You have to understand that it serves the federal government extremely well with this thing on the overlook being part of a terrorism plot. A bona fide domestic threat would go a long way toward deflecting public attention and easing the pressure in other areas. The war's gone to shit, the election was a disaster. You've got the Middle East, the price of a gallon of gasoline and a lame-duck president's approval ratings. The list goes on and on and there would be an opportunity here for redemption.

A chance to make up for past mistakes. A chance to shift public attention and opinion."

Bosch nodded.

"Are you saying that they might try to keep this thing going, maybe even exaggerate the threat?"

"I'm not saying anything, Detective. I am just trying to broaden your perspective. A case like this, you have to be aware of the political landscape. You can't be running around like a bull in a china shop—which in the past has been your specialty."

Bosch nodded.

"Not only that, you have local politics to consider," the chief continued. "You have a man on the city council who lies in wait for me."

The chief was talking about Irvin Irving, a longtime commander in the department whom the chief had forced out. He'd run for a city council seat and won. He was now the department's and the chief's harshest critic.

"Irving?" Bosch said. "He's just one vote on the council."

"He knows a lot of secrets. It's allowed him to start building a political base. He sent me a message after the election. It was just two words. 'Expect me.' Don't turn this into something he can use, Detective."

The chief stood up, ready to go.

"Think about it and be careful," he said. "Remember, no reflux. No blowback."

"Yes, sir."

The chief turned and nodded to his driver. The man went to the door and held it open for his charge.

THIRTEEN

BOSCH DIDN'T SPEAK until they were out of the parking lot. He decided that by this time of day the Hollywood Freeway would be overrun by the morning commute and surface streets would be better. He believed that Sunset was the fastest way downtown.

Ferras only made it two blocks before asking what had happened in the doughnut shop.

"Don't worry, Ignacio. We both still have our jobs."

"Then, what happened?"

"He said you were right. I shouldn't have jumped command. But he said he would make some calls and try to open things up with the feds."

"Then I guess we'll see."

"Yeah, we'll see."

They drove in silence for a while until Bosch brought up his partner's plan to ask for a new assignment.

"You still going to talk to the lieutenant?"

Ferras paused before answering. He was uncomfortable with the question.

"I don't know, Harry. I still think it would be best. Best for both of us. Maybe you work best with female partners."

Bosch almost laughed. Ferras didn't know Kiz Rider, his last partner. She never went along to get along with Harry. Like Ferras, she objected every time Bosch went alpha dog on her. He was about to set Ferras straight, when his cell phone started buzzing and he pulled it out of his pocket. It was Lieutenant Gandle.

"Harry, where are you?"

His voice was louder than usual and more urgent. He was excited about something and Bosch wondered if he had already heard about the Donut Hole meeting. Had the chief betrayed him?

"I'm on Sunset. We're heading in."

"Did you pass Silver Lake yet?"

"Not yet."

"Good. Head up to Silver Lake. Go to the rec center at the bottom of the reservoir."

"What's going on, Lieutenant?"

"The Kent car's been located. Hadley and his people are already out there setting up the CP. They've requested the investigators on scene."

"Hadley? Why's he there? Why is there a command post?"

"Hadley's office got the tip and checked it out before deciding to clue us in. The car is parked in front of a house belonging to a person of interest. They want you on the scene."

"'Person of interest'? What's that mean?"

"The house is the residence of a person the OHS has an interest in. Some sort of suspected terrorist sympathizer. I don't have all the details. Just get there, Harry."

"All right. We're on the way."

"Call me and let me know what's happening. If you need me out there just say the word."

Of course, Gandle didn't really want to leave the office and go to the scene. That would set him back on his daily management duties and paperwork. Bosch closed the phone and tried to pick up speed but the traffic was too thick for him to get anywhere. He filled Ferras in on what little he knew from the phone call.

"What about the FBI?" Ferras asked.

"What about them?"

"Do they know?"

"I didn't ask."

"What about the meeting at ten?"

"I guess we'll worry about that at ten."

In ten minutes they finally got to Silver Lake Boulevard and Bosch turned north. This part of the city took its name from the Silver Lake Reservoir which sat in the middle of the largely middle-class neighborhood of bungalows and post–World War Two homes with views of the man-made lake.

As they approached the recreation center Bosch saw two shiny black SUVs that he recognized as the signature vehicles of the OHS. Apparently, he thought, there was never much trouble getting funding for a unit that supposedly hunted terrorists. There were two patrol cars and a city sanitation truck as well. Bosch parked behind one of the patrol cars and he and Ferras got out.

There was a group of ten men in black

fatigues—also distinctive to the OHS— gathered around the fold-down rear gate of one of the SUVs. Bosch approached them and Ferras trailed a couple of steps behind. Their presence was immediately noticed and the crowd parted and there was Captain Don Hadley sitting on the gate. Bosch had never met him but had seen him often enough on television. He was a large, red-faced man with sandy hair. He was about forty years old and looked like he had been in the gym working out for half of them. His ruddy complexion gave him the look of someone who had overexerted himself or was holding his breath.

"Bosch?" Hadley asked. "Ferras?"

"I'm Bosch. This is Ferras."

"Fellas, good to have you here. I think we're going to tie your case up for you in a bow in short order. We're just waiting on one of my guys to bring the warrant and then we go in."

He stood up and signaled to one of his men. Hadley had a definite air of confidence about him.

"Perez, check on that warrant, will you? I'm tired of waiting. Then check the OP and see what's happening up there."

He then turned back to Bosch and Ferras.

"Walk with me, men."

Hadley headed away from the group and Bosch and Ferras followed. He led them to the back of the sanitation truck so he could talk to them away from the cluster of other men. The captain adopted a command pose, putting his foot up on the back end of the truck and resting his elbow on his knee. Bosch noticed that he carried his sidearm in a leg holster that was strapped around his thick right thigh. Like an Old West gunslinger except he was carrying a semi-automatic. He was chewing gum and not trying to hide it.

Bosch had heard many stories about Hadley. He now had the feeling that he was about to become part of one.

"I wanted you men to be here for this," Hadley said.

"What exactly is this, Captain?" Bosch replied.

Hadley clapped his hands together before speaking.

"We've located your Chrysler Three Hundred approximately two and a half blocks from here on a street bordering the reservoir. The plate matches the BOLO and I eyeballed the vehicle myself. It's the car we've been looking for."

Bosch nodded. That part was good, he thought. What's the rest?

"The vehicle is parked in front of a home owned by a man named Ramin Samir," Hadley continued. "He's a guy we've been keeping our eye on for a few years now. A real person of interest to us, you might say."

The name was familiar to Bosch but he couldn't place it at first.

"Why is he of interest, Captain?" he asked.

"Mr. Samir is a known supporter of religious organizations that want to hurt Americans and damage our interests. What's worse than that is that he teaches our young people to hate their own country."

That last part jogged Bosch's memory and he put things together.

He could not recall which Middle Eastern country he was from, but Bosch remembered that Ramin Samir was a former visiting professor of international politics at USC who had gained widespread notice for espousing anti-American sentiment in the classroom and in the media.

He was making media ripples before the

9/11 domestic terrorist attacks. Afterward, the ripples became a wave. He openly postulated that the attacks were warranted because of U.S. intrusion and aggression all around the globe. He was able to parlay the attention this brought him into a position as the media go-to guy for the ever-ready anti-American quote or sound bite. He denigrated U.S. policies toward Israel, objected to the military action in Afghanistan and called the war in Iraq nothing more than an oil grab.

Samir's role as agent provocateur was good for a few years of guest shots on the cable-news debate programs, where everybody tends to yell at one another. He was a perfect foil for both the right and the left and always willing to get up at 4 a.m. to make the Sunday-morning programs in the East.

Meantime, he used his soapbox and celebrity status to help start and fund a number of organizations on and off campus that were quickly accused by conservative interest groups and in newspaper investigations of being connected, at least tangentially, to terrorist organizations and anti-American jihads. Some even suggested that there were links to the grand master of all terror, Osama bin Laden. But while Samir was often investigated, he was never charged with any crime. He was, however, fired by USC on a technicality—he had not stated that his opinions were his own and not those of the school when he wrote an op-ed piece for the *Los Angeles Times* that suggested the Iraq war was an American-planned genocide of Muslims.

Samir's fifteen minutes ran their course. He was eventually discounted in the media as a narcissistic provocateur who made outlandish statements in order to draw attention to himself rather than to thoughtfully comment on the issues of the day. After all, he had even named one of his organizations the YMCA—for Young Muslim Cause in America—just so the long-established youth organization with the same internationally recognized initials would file an attention-getting lawsuit.

Samir's star waned and he dropped from public sight. Bosch could not remember the last time he had seen him on the box or in the paper. But all the rhetoric aside, the fact that Samir was never charged with a crime during a period when the climate in the United States was hot with fear of the unknown and the desire for vengeance always indicated to

Bosch that there was nothing there. If there had been fire behind the smoke, then Ramin Samir would be in a prison cell or behind a fence at Guantánamo Bay. But here he was, living in Silver Lake, and Bosch was skeptical of Captain Hadley's claims.

"I remember this guy," he said. "He was just a talker, Captain. There was never any solid link between Samir and—"

Hadley held up a finger like a teacher demanding silence.

"Never a solid link *established*," he corrected. "But that doesn't mean anything. This guy raises money for the Palestinian Jihad and other Muslim causes."

"The Palestinian Jihad?" Bosch asked. "What is that? And what Muslim causes? Are you saying Muslim causes can't be legit?"

"Look, all I'm saying is that this is a bad dude and he's got a car that was used in a murder and zesium heist sitting right in front of his house."

"Cesium," Ferras said. "It was cesium that was stolen."

Not used to being corrected, Hadley narrowed his eyes and stared at Ferras for a moment before speaking.

"Whatever. It's not going to make much

difference what you call it, son, if he dumps it into the reservoir across the street or is in that house putting it in a bomb while we're sitting here waiting on a warrant."

"The FBI didn't say anything about it being a water-borne threat," Bosch said.

Hadley shook his head.

"Doesn't matter. Bottom line is that it's a threat. I'm sure the FBI said that. Well, the bureau can talk about it. We're going to *do* something about it."

Bosch stepped back, trying to draw some fresh air into the discussion. This was moving too quickly.

"So you're going to go in?" he asked.

Hadley was working his jaw in quick powerful bites of the gum. He seemed not to notice the strong odor of garbage emanating from the back of the truck.

"You're damn right we're going to go in," he said. "Just as soon as that warrant gets here."

"You got a judge to sign a warrant that's based on a stolen car being parked in front of the house?" Bosch asked.

Hadley signaled to one of his men.

"Bring the bags, Perez," he called. Then to Bosch he said, "No, that's not all we got. Today's trash day, Detective. I sent the garbage truck up the street and a couple of my men emptied the two cans that were in front of Samir's house. Perfectly legal, as you know. And lookee at what we got."

Perez hustled over with the plastic evidence bags and handed them to Hadley.

"Captain, I checked the OP," Perez said. "Still quiet up there."

"Thank you, Perez."

Hadley took the bags and turned back to Bosch and Ferras. Perez went back to the SUV.

"Our observation post is a guy in a tree," Hadley said with a smile. "He'll let us know if anybody makes a move up there before we're ready."

He handed Bosch the bags. Two of them contained black woolen ski masks. The third contained a slip of paper with a hand-drawn map on it. Bosch looked closely at it. It was a series of crisscrossing lines with two of them marked as Arrowhead and Mulholland. Once he registered these he could tell the map was a fairly accurate rendering of the neighborhood where Stanley Kent had lived and died.

Bosch handed the bags back and shook his head.

"Captain, I think you should hold up."

Hadley looked shocked by the suggestion.

"Hold up? We're not holding up. If this guy and his pals contaminate the reservoir with that poison, do you think the people of this city are going to accept that we held up to make sure we dotted every *i* and crossed every *t*? We're not holding up."

He underlined his resolve by taking the gum out of his mouth and throwing it into the back of the sanitation truck. He took his foot off the bumper and started heading back to his crew but then made a sudden U-turn and came back directly to Bosch.

"As far as I'm concerned we've got the leader of a terrorist cell operating out of that house and we're going to go in and shut it down. What's your problem with that, Detective Bosch?"

"It's too easy, that's my problem. It's not about us dotting every *i* because that's what the killers already did. This was a carefully planned crime, Captain. They wouldn't have just left the car in front of the house or put this stuff in the trash cans. Think about it."

Bosch held there and watched Hadley work it over for a few moments. He then shook his head.

"Maybe the car wasn't left there," he said. "Maybe they still plan to use it as part of the delivery. There are a lot of variables, Bosch. Things we don't know. We're still going in. We laid it all out to the judge and he said we have probable cause. That's good enough for me. We've got a no-knock warrant coming and we're going to use it."

Bosch refused to give up.

"Where did the tip come from, Captain? How did you find the car?"

Hadley's jaw started working but then he remembered he had tossed his gum.

"One of my sources," he said. "We've been building an intelligence network in this city for almost four years. Today it's paying off."

"Are you telling me you know who the source is or did it come in anonymously?"

Hadley waved his hands in a dismissive manner.

"Doesn't matter," he said. "The info was good. That's the car up there. There's no doubt about that."

He pointed in the direction of the reservoir. Bosch knew by Hadley's sidestepping that the tip was anonymous, the hallmark of a setup.

"Captain, I urge you to stand down," he said. "There is something not right about this. It's too simple and this wasn't a simple plan. It's some sort of misdirection and we need to figure —"

"We're not standing down, Detective. Lives could hang in the balance."

Bosch shook his head. He wasn't going to get through to Hadley. The man believed he was poised at the edge of some sort of victory that would redeem every mistake he had ever made.

"Where's the FBI?" Bosch asked. "Shouldn't they be —"

"We don't need the FBI," Hadley said, getting in Bosch's face again. "We have the training, the equipment and the skills. What's more, we have the balls. And for once we're going to take care of what's in our own backyard ourselves."

He gestured to the ground as if the place where he stood was the last battlefield between the bureau and the LAPD.

"What about the chief?" Bosch tried. "Does he know? I was just —"

Bosch stopped, remembering the chief's

admonishment about keeping their meeting at the Donut Hole to themselves.

"You were just what?" Hadley asked.

"I just want to know if he knows and approves."

"The chief has given me full authority to run my unit. Do you call the chief every time you go out and make an arrest?"

He turned and marched imperiously back to his men, leaving Bosch and Ferras to watch him go.

"Uh-oh," Ferras said.

"Yeah," Bosch said.

Bosch stepped away from the back of the foul-smelling sanitation truck and pulled out his phone. He scrolled through his directory to Rachel Walling's name. He had just pressed the call button when Hadley was there in his face again. Bosch hadn't heard him coming.

"Detective! Who are you calling?"

Bosch didn't hesitate.

"My lieutenant. He told me to update him after we got here."

"No cellular or radio transmissions. They could be monitoring."

"They who?"

"Give me the phone."

"Captain?"

"Give me the phone or I will have it taken from you. We're not going to compromise this operation."

Bosch closed the phone without ending the call. If he was lucky Walling would answer the call and be listening. She might be able to put it together and get the warning. The bureau might even be able to triangulate the cell transmission and get to Silver Lake before things went completely wrong.

He handed the phone to Hadley, who then turned to Ferras.

"Your phone, Detective."

"Sir, my wife is eight months pregnant and I need—"

"Your phone, Detective. You are either with us or against us."

Hadley held his hand out and Ferras reluctantly took his phone from his belt and gave it to him.

Hadley marched over to one of the SUVs, opened the passenger door and put the two phones into the glove box. He slammed the compartment shut with authority and looked back at Bosch and Ferras as if challenging them to try to retrieve their phones.

The captain's attention was then distracted

when a third black SUV pulled into the lot. The driver gave the captain a thumbs-up. Hadley then pointed a finger into the air and started a twirling motion.

"All right, everybody," he called out. "We have the warrant and you know the plan. Perez, call air support and get us the eye in the sky. The rest of you warriors mount up! We're going in."

Bosch watched with growing dread as the members of the OHS chambered rounds in their weapons and put on helmets with face shields. Two of the men began putting on space suits, as they had been designated the radiation-containment team.

"This is crazy," Ferras said in a whisper.

"Charlie don't surf," Bosch replied.

"What?"

"Nothing. Before your time."

FOURTEEN

THE SLICK BANKED OVER a thirty-acre rubber plantation and put down in the LZ with the usual spine-compressing final drop. Hari Kari Bosch, Bunk Simmons, Ted Furness and Gabe Finley rolled out into the mud and Captain Gillette was there waiting for them, holding his helmet on top of his head so he wouldn't lose it in the rotor wash. The chopper labored as it pulled its skids out of the mud—it was the first dry day after six days of rain—and took off, following the line of an irrigation canal back in the direction of III Corps HQ.

"Walk with me, men," Gillette said.

Bosch and Simmons had been in country long enough to have nicknames but Furness and Finley were fresh and strictly OJT— on-the-job training—and Bosch knew they were scared shitless. This was going to be their first drop and nothing they taught you back at tunnel school in San Diego could prepare you for the sights, sounds and smells of the real thing.

The captain led them to a card table set up under the command tent and outlined his plan. The tunnel system under Ben Cat was extensive and needed to be taken out as part of a first-wave attempt to take control of the village above. Already the casualties from sappers and sneak attacks inside the camp perimeter were mounting. The captain explained that he was getting his ass eaten out on a daily basis by III Corps command. He didn't mention anything about being bothered by the dead and wounded he was losing. They were replaceable but his favor with the colonel at III Corps was not.

The plan was a simple crimp operation. The captain unrolled a map drawn with the aid of villagers who had been in the tunnels. He pointed to four separate spider holes and said the four tunnel rats would go down simultaneously and force the VC in the tunnels toward a fifth hole, where the warriors of Tropic Lightning would be on top waiting to massacre them. Along the way Bosch and his fellow rats would set charges and the operation would finish with the implosion of the entire tunnel system.

The plan was simple enough until they got down there in the darkness and the labyrinth didn't match the map they had studied on the card table under the tent. Four went down but only one came back up alive. Tropic Lightning got zero kills that day. And that was the day that Bosch knew the war was lost—for him, at least. That was when he knew that men of rank often fought battles with enemies that were inside.

BOSCH AND FERRAS RODE IN THE BACKSEAT of Captain's SUV. Perez drove and Hadley rode shotgun, wearing a radio headset so he could command the operation. The vehicle's radio speaker was on loud and set to the operation's back-channel frequency—one that would not be found listed in any public directories.

They were third in line in the entourage of black SUVs. Half a block from the target

house Perez braked to let the other two vehicles move in as planned.

Bosch leaned forward between the front
seats so he could see better through the
windshield. Each of the other SUVs had four
men riding on runners on either side. The vehicles picked up speed and then turned
sharply toward the Samir house. One went
down the driveway of the small Craftsman-
style bungalow toward the rear yard while the
other jumped the curb and crossed the front
lawn. One of the OHS men lost his grip when
the heavy vehicle impacted the curb and he
went tumbling across the lawn.

The others leaped from the runners and
moved toward the front door. Bosch assumed
the same thing was happening at the back
door. He didn't agree with the plan but admired its precision. There was a loud pop-
ping sound when the front door was breached
with an explosive device. And almost immediately there was another from the rear.

"All right, move up," Hadley commanded
Perez.

As they drove up, the radio came alive with
reports from inside the house.

"We're inside!"

"We're in the back!"

"Front room clear! We—"

The voice was cut off by the sound of automatic gunfire.

"Shots fired!"

"We've got—"

"Shots fired!"

Bosch heard more gunfire but not over the radio. They were now close enough for him to hear it live. Perez jammed the SUV into park at an angle crossing the street in front of the house. All four doors opened at once as they jumped out, leaving the doors open behind them and the radio blaring.

"All clear! All clear!"

"One suspect down. We need medical for one suspect down. We need medical!"

It was all over in less than twenty seconds.

Bosch ran across the lawn behind Hadley and Perez. Ferras was to his left side. They entered through the front door with weapons out and up. Immediately they were met by one of Hadley's men. Above the right pocket of his fatigue shirt was the name Peck.

"We're clear! We're clear!"

Bosch dropped his weapon to his side but he didn't holster it. He looked around. It was a sparely furnished living room. He smelled the exploded gunpowder and saw blue smoke hanging in the air.

"What have we got?" Hadley demanded.

"One down, one in custody," Peck said. "Back here."

They followed Peck down a short hallway to a room with woven-grass mats on the floor. A man Bosch recognized as Ramin Samir was on his back on the floor, blood from two chest wounds flowing over a cream-colored robe onto the floor and one of the mats. A young woman in a matching robe was lying facedown and whimpering, her hands cuffed behind her back.

Bosch saw a revolver on the floor by the open drawer of a small cabinet with lit votive candles on top of it. The gun was about eighteen inches from where Samir was lying.

"He went for the gun and we took him down," Peck said.

Bosch looked down at Samir. He wasn't conscious and his chest was rising and falling in a broken rhythm.

"He's circling the drain," Hadley said. "What have we found?"

"So far no materials," Peck said. "We're bringing in the equipment now."

"All right, let's get the car checked," Hadley ordered. "And get her out of here."

While two OHS men raised the crying woman up and carried her out of the room like a battering ram Hadley headed back out of the house to the curb, where the Chrysler 300 awaited. Bosch and Ferras followed.

They looked into the car but didn't touch it. Bosch noticed that it was unlocked. He bent down to look in through the passenger-side windows.

"Keys are in it," he said.

He pulled a pair of latex gloves from his coat pocket, stretched them and put them on.

"Let's get a reading on it first, Bosch," Hadley said.

The captain signaled one of his men who was carrying a radiation monitor over. The man swept the device over the car and only picked up a few low pops by the trunk.

"We could have something right here," Hadley said.

"I doubt it," Bosch said. "It's not here."

He opened the driver-side door and leaned in.

"Bosch, wait—"

Bosch pushed the trunk button before Hadley could finish. He heard the pneumatic pop and the trunk came open. He backed out of the car and walked to the rear. The trunk was empty, but Bosch saw the same four indentations he had seen earlier in the trunk of Stanley Kent's Porsche.

"It's gone," Hadley said, looking into the trunk. "They must've already made the transfer."

"Yeah, long before the car was brought here."

Bosch looked Hadley squarely in the eyes.

"This was a misdirection, Captain. I told you that."

Hadley moved toward Bosch so he could speak without his whole crew hearing him. But he was intercepted by Peck.

"Captain?"

"What?" Hadley barked.

"The suspect went code seven."

"Then call off the paramedics and call the coroner."

"Yes, sir. The house is clear. No materials and the monitors are picking up no signature."

Hadley glanced at Bosch and then quickly looked back at Peck.

"Tell them to check the place again," he ordered. "The fucker went for a gun. He had to have been hiding something. Tear the place apart if you have to. Especially that room—it looks like a meeting place for terrorists."

"It's a prayer room," Bosch said. "And maybe the guy went for the gun because he was scared shitless when people came busting through the doors."

Peck hadn't moved. He was listening to Bosch.

"Go!" Hadley ordered. "Tear the fucker apart! The material was in a lead container. Just because you got no reading doesn't mean it's not in there!"

Peck hustled back to the house and Hadley turned his stare to Bosch.

"We need Forensics to process the car," Bosch said. "And I don't have a phone to make the call."

"Go get your phone and make the call."

Bosch went back to the SUV. He watched the woman who had been in the house being placed in the back of the SUV parked on the

lawn. She was still crying and Bosch assumed the tears wouldn't stop anytime soon.
For Samir now, herself later.

As he leaned through the door of Hadley's SUV he realized that the vehicle was
still running. He turned off the engine, then
opened the glove compartment and took
out the two phones. He opened and checked
his to see if the call to Rachel Walling was
still connected. It wasn't and he didn't know
if the call had gone through in the first
place.

When he turned from the door Hadley was
standing there. They were away from the others and no one would hear them.

"Bosch, if you try to make trouble for this
unit I will make trouble for you. You understand?"

Bosch studied him for a moment before
responding.

"Sure, Captain. I'm glad you're thinking
about the unit."

"I have connections that go all the way up
and right out of this department. I can hurt
you."

"Thanks for the advice."

Bosch started to walk away from him but

then stopped. He wanted to say something but hesitated.

"What?" Hadley said. "Say it."

"I was just thinking about a captain I once worked for. This was a long time ago and in another place. He kept making all the wrong moves and his fuckups kept costing people their lives. Good people. So eventually it had to stop. That captain ended up getting fragged in the latrine by some of his own men. The story was that afterward they couldn't separate his parts from the shit."

Bosch walked away but Hadley stopped him.

"What's that supposed to mean? Is that a threat?"

"No, it's a story."

"And you're calling that guy in there *good* people? Let me tell you, a guy like that stood up and cheered when the planes hit the buildings."

Bosch kept walking as he answered.

"I don't know what kind of people he was, Captain. I just know he wasn't part of this and he was set up just like you. If you figure out who it was who tipped you to the car, let me know. It might help us."

Bosch walked over to Ferras and gave him back his phone. He told his partner to remain on the scene to supervise the forensic analysis of the Chrysler.

"Where are you going, Harry?"

"Downtown."

"What about the meeting with the bureau?"

Bosch didn't check his watch.

"We missed it. Call me if SID comes up with anything."

Bosch left him there and started walking down the street toward the recreation center, where the car was parked.

"Bosch, where are you going?" Hadley called. "You're not done here!"

Bosch waved without looking back. He kept walking. When he was halfway back to the rec center the first TV truck passed him on its way to Samir's house.

FIFTEEN

BOSCH WAS HOPING TO GET to the federal building downtown before news of the raid on Ramin Samir's house did. He had tried to call
Rachel Walling but got no answer. He knew
that she might be at the Tactical Intelligence
location but he didn't know where that was.
He only knew where the federal building was
and he was banking on the idea that the
growing size and importance of the investigation would dictate that it be directed from
the main building and not a secret satellite
office.

He entered the building through the law
enforcement door and told the U.S. marshal

who checked his ID that he was going up to
the FBI. He took the elevator up to the fourteenth floor and was greeted by Brenner as
soon as the doors came open. The word that
Bosch was in the building had obviously been
sent up from below.

"I thought you got the message," Brenner
said.

"What message?"

"That the status conference was can-
celed."

"I think I should've gotten the message as
soon as you people showed up. There never
was going to be a status conference, was
there?"

Brenner ignored the question.

"Bosch, what do you want?"

"I want to see Agent Walling."

"I'm her partner. Anything you want to tell
her, you can tell me."

"Only her. I want to talk to her."

Brenner studied him for a moment.

"Come with me," he finally said.

He didn't wait for a reply. He used a clip-on
ID card to open a door and Bosch followed
him through. They went down a long hallway
and Brenner threw questions over his shoulder as he walked.

"Where's your partner?" he asked.

"He's back at the crime scene," Bosch said.

It wasn't a lie. Bosch just neglected to say which crime scene Ferras was at.

"Besides," he added, "I thought it would be safer for him there. I don't want you people leaning on him to get to me."

Brenner suddenly stopped, pivoted sharply and was in Bosch's face.

"Do you know what you are doing, Bosch? You're compromising an investigation that could have far-reaching implications. Where is the witness?"

Bosch shrugged as if to say his response was obvious.

"Where's Alicia Kent?"

Brenner shook his head but didn't answer.

"Wait in here," he said. "I'll go get Agent Walling."

Brenner opened a door that had the number 1411 on it and stepped back for Bosch to enter. As he stepped through the door Bosch saw that it was a small, windowless interview room similar to the one he had spent time in that morning with Jesse Mitford. Bosch was suddenly shoved into the room from behind and he turned just in time to see Brenner out in the hallway pulling the door closed.

"Hey!"

Bosch grabbed for the doorknob but it was too late. The door was locked from the outside. He pounded twice on it but knew that Brenner was not about to open it. He turned away and looked at the small space he was confined in. Similar to those at the LAPD, the interview room contained only three items of furniture. A small square table and two chairs. Assuming there was a camera somewhere he raised his hand and shot his middle finger into the air. He gave his hand a twirl to emphasize the message.

Bosch pulled one of the chairs out and sat down on it backwards, ready to wait them out. He took his cell phone out and opened it. He knew that if they were watching him they wouldn't want him calling out and reporting his situation—it could be embarrassing for the bureau. But when he looked at the screen there was no signal. It was a safe room. Radio signals could not get out or in. Leave it to the feds, Bosch thought. They think of everything.

A long twenty minutes went by and then the door finally opened. Rachel Walling stepped in. She closed the door, took the chair opposite Bosch and quietly sat down.

"Sorry, Harry, I was over at Tactical."

"What the fuck, Rachel. You people hold cops against their will now?"

She looked surprised.

"What are you talking about?"

"What are you talking about?" Bosch repeated in a mocking voice. "Your partner locked me in here."

"It wasn't locked when I came in. Try it now."

Bosch waved all the bullshit away.

"Forget it. I don't have time to play games. What's going on with the investigation?"

She pursed her lips as if considering how to respond.

"What's going on is that you and your department have been running around like thieves in a jewelry store, smashing every goddamn case in sight. You can't tell the glass from the diamonds."

Bosch nodded.

"So you know about Ramin Samir."

"Who doesn't? It's already on I-Missed-It News. What happened up there?"

"A class-A fuckup is what happened. We were set up. OHS was set up."

"Sounds like somebody was."

Bosch leaned across the table.

"But it means something, Rachel. The people who put the OHS onto Samir knew who he was and that he'd make an easy target. They left the Kents' car right in front of his house because they knew we'd end up spinning our wheels."

"It also could have worked as a payback to Samir."

"What do you mean?"

"All those years he was on CNN fanning the flames. He could've been seen as hurting their cause because he was giving the enemy a face and heightening American anger and resolve."

Bosch didn't get it.

"I thought agitation was one of their tools. I thought they loved this guy."

"Maybe. It's hard to say."

Bosch wasn't sure what she was trying to say. But when Rachel leaned across the table he suddenly could see how angry she was.

"Now let's talk about you and how you have been single-handedly fucking things up since before the car was even found."

"What are you talking about? I'm trying to solve a homicide. That's my—"

"Yes, trying to solve a homicide at the possible cost of endangering the entire city with this petty, selfish and self-righteous insistence on—"

"Come on, Rachel, don't you think I have an idea about what could be at stake here?"

She shook her head.

"Not if you are holding back a key witness from us. Don't you see what you are doing? You have no idea where this investigation is headed because you've been busy hiding witnesses and sucker punching agents."

Bosch leaned back, clearly surprised.

"Is that what Maxwell said, that I sucker punched him?"

"It doesn't matter what he said. We are trying to control a potentially devastating situation here and I don't understand why you are making the moves you are making."

Bosch nodded.

"That makes sense," he said. "You shut somebody out of his own investigation and it stands to reason you won't know what he is up to."

She held her hands up as if to stop an on-coming train.

"Okay, let's just stop everything right here. Talk to me, Harry. What is your problem?"

Bosch looked at her and then up at the ceiling. He studied the upper corners of the room and dropped his eyes back to hers.

"You want to talk? Let's take a walk out-side, then we can talk."

She didn't hesitate.

"Okay, fine," she said. "Let's walk and talk. And then you'll give me Mitford."

Walling got up and moved to the door. Bosch saw her quickly glance up at an air-conditioning grille high on the back wall and it confirmed for him that they were on cam-era.

She opened the unlocked door and Brenner and another agent were waiting in the hallway.

"We're going to take a little walk," Walling said. "Alone."

"Have a great time," Brenner said. "We'll be in here trying to track the cesium, maybe save a few lives."

Walling and Bosch didn't respond. She led him down the hall. Just as they were at the door to the elevator hall Bosch heard a voice from behind him.

"Hey, buddy!"

He turned just in time to take Agent Maxwell's shoulder in the chest. He was driven into the wall and held up against it.

"You're a little outnumbered this time, aren't you, Bosch!"

"Stop!" Walling shouted. "Cliff, stop it!"

Bosch brought his arm up around Maxwell's head and was going to pull him down into a headlock. But Walling waded in and pulled Maxwell away and then pushed him back up the hallway.

"Cliff, get back! Get away!"

Maxwell started moving backwards up the hall. He pointed a finger over Walling's shoulder at Bosch.

"Get out of my building, motherfucker! Get out and stay out!"

Walling shoved him into the first open office and then closed the door on him. By then several other agents had come into the hallway to see what the commotion was about.

"It's all over," Walling announced. "Everybody just go back to work."

She came back to Bosch and pushed him through the door to the elevator.

"You okay?"

"Only hurts when I breathe."

"Son of a bitch! That guy is getting out of control."

They took the elevator down to the garage level and walked from there up an incline and out onto Los Angeles Street. She turned right and he caught up. They were heading away from the noise of the freeway. She checked her watch and then pointed toward an office building of modern design and construction.

"There's decent coffee in there," she said. "But I don't want to take a lot of time."

It was the new Social Security Administration building.

"Another federal building," Bosch sighed. "Agent Maxwell might think that's his, too."

"Can you drop that, please?"

He shrugged.

"I'm just surprised Maxwell even admitted we came back to the house."

"Why wouldn't he?"

"Because I figured he was posted on the house because he was already in the doghouse for being a fuckup. Why admit that we got the drop on him and have to stay in there longer?"

Walling shook her head.

"You don't understand," she said. "First of all, Maxwell has been wound a little tight lately but no one in Tactical Intelligence is in the doghouse. The work is too important to have any fuckups on the team. Secondly, he didn't care what anyone would think. What he did think was that it was important for everyone to know about the way *you're* fucking things up."

He tried another direction.

"Let me ask you something. Do they know about you and me over there? Our history, I mean."

"It would be hard for them not to know after Echo Park. But, Harry, never mind all of that. That is not important today. What is wrong with you? We've got enough cesium out there to shut down an airport and you don't seem all that concerned. You are looking at this like it's a murder. Yes, a man is dead but that isn't what this is about. It's a heist, Harry. Get it? They wanted the cesium and now they've got it. And it would help us if maybe we could talk to the only known witness. So where is he?"

"He's safe. Where's Alicia Kent? And where's her husband's partner?"

"They're safe. The partner is being questioned here and we're keeping the wife at Tactical until we are sure we have everything there is to get from her."

"She's not going to be very helpful. She couldn't—"

"That's where you are wrong. She's already been quite helpful."

Bosch couldn't hold back the look of surprise in his eyes.

"How? She said she didn't even see their faces."

"She didn't. But she heard a name. When they were speaking to each other, she heard a name."

"What name? She didn't say this before."

Walling nodded.

"And that is why you should turn over your witness. We have people who have one expertise: getting information from witnesses. We can get things that you are unable to get. We got them from her, we can get them from him."

Bosch felt his face turning red.

"What was the name this master interrogator got from her?"

She shook her head.

"We're not trading, Harry. This is a case involving national security. You're on the outside. And by the way, that's not going to change no matter who you get your police chief to call."

Bosch knew then that his meeting at the Donut Hole had been for nothing. Even the chief was on the outside looking in. Whatever name Alicia Kent gave up, it must have lit up the federal scoreboard like Times Square.

"All I've got is my witness," he said. "I'll trade you straight up for the name."

"Why do you want the name? You're not going to get anywhere near this guy."

"Because I want to know."

She folded her arms across her chest and thought about things for a moment. Finally, she looked at him.

"You first," she said.

Bosch hesitated while he studied her eyes. Six months earlier he would have trusted her with his life. Now things had changed. Bosch wasn't so sure.

"I stashed him at my place," he said. "I think you remember where that is."

She pulled a phone from her blazer pocket and opened it to make a call.

"Wait a second there, Agent Walling," he said. "What was the name Alicia Kent gave you?"

"Sorry, Harry."

"We had a deal."

"National security, sorry."

She started punching in a number on her cell. Bosch nodded. He had called it right.

"I lied," he said. "He's not at my place."

She slapped the phone closed.

"What is with you?" she asked angrily, her voice getting shrill. "We're running more than fourteen hours behind the cesium. Do you realize it may already be in a device? It may already be —"

Bosch stepped in close to her.

"Give me the name and I'll give you the witness."

"All *right!*"

She pushed him away. He knew she was angry with herself for being caught in the lie. It was the second time in less than twelve hours.

"She said she heard the name Moby, okay? She didn't think anything about it at the time because she didn't realize it was actually a name she had heard."

"Okay, who is Moby?"

"There is a Syrian terrorist named Momar Azim Nassar. He is believed to be in this country. He is known by friends and associates as Moby. We don't know why, but he does happen to resemble the performer named Moby."

"Who?"

"Never mind. Not your generation."

"But you are sure she heard this name?"

"Yes. She gave us the name. And I have now given it to you. Now, where is the witness?"

"Just hold on. You already lied to me once."

Bosch pulled out his phone and was about to call his partner when he remembered that Ferras would still be at the Silver Lake crime scene and be unable to provide what he needed. He opened the directory on the phone, found the number for Kiz Rider and pushed the call button.

Rider answered immediately. Bosch's number had showed up on caller ID.

"Hello, Harry. You've been busy today."

"The chief tell you that?"

"I've got a few sources. What's up?"

Bosch spoke while staring at Walling and watching the anger darken her eyes.

"I need a favor from my old partner. You still carry that laptop with you to work?"

"Of course. What favor?"

"Can you get the *New York Times* archives on that computer?"

"I can."

"All right. I have a name. I want you to check to see if it's been in any stories."

"Hold on. I have to go online."

Several seconds went by. Bosch's phone started to beep because he was getting another call. But he stayed with Rider and soon she was ready.

"What's the name?"

Bosch put his hand over the phone and asked Walling the full name of the Syrian terrorist again. He then repeated it to Rider and waited.

"Yeah, multiple hits," she said. "Going back eight years."

"Give me a rundown."

Bosch waited.

"Uh, just a bunch of stuff from the Middle East. He's suspected of involvement in a number of abductions and bombings and so on. He's connected to al Qaeda, according to federal sources."

"What's the most recent story say?"

"Uh, let's see. It's about a bus bombing in Beirut. Sixteen people killed. This is January third, two thousand four. Nothing after that."

"Does it give any nicknames or aliases?"

"Um . . . no. I don't see anything."

"Okay, thanks. I'll call you later."

"Wait a minute. Harry?"

"What? I have to go."

"Listen, I just want to tell you, be careful out there, okay? This is a whole different league you're playing in with this."

"Okay, I got it," Bosch said. "I gotta go."

Bosch ended the call and looked at Rachel.

"There's nothing in the *New York Times* about this guy being in this country."

"Because it's not known. That is why Alicia Kent's information was so genuine."

"What do you mean? You take her word for it that the guy's in this country just because she heard a word that might not even be a name?"

She folded her arms. She was losing her patience.

"No, Harry, we *know* he's in this country. We have video of him checking out the Port of Los Angeles last August. We just didn't get there in time to grab him. We believe he was with another al Qaeda operative, named Muhammad El-Fayed. They've somehow slipped into this country—hell, the border's a sieve—and who knows what they've got planned."

"And you think they have the cesium?"

"We don't know that. But the intelligence on El-Fayed is that he smokes unfiltered Turkish cigarettes and—"

"The ashes on the toilet."

She nodded.

"That's right. They're still being analyzed but the betting in the office is running eight to one that it was a Turkish cigarette."

Bosch nodded and suddenly felt foolish about the moves he had been making, the information he had held back.

"We put the witness in the Mark Twain Hotel on Wilcox," he said. "Room three-oh-three under the name Stephen King."

"Cute."

"And, Rachel?"

"What?"

"He told us he heard the shooter call out to Allah before he pulled the trigger."

She looked at him with the eyes of judgment as she opened her phone again. She pushed a single button and spoke to Bosch while waiting for the connection.

"You better hope we get to these people before—"

She cut off when her call was picked up. She delivered the information without identifying herself or giving any sort of greeting.

"He's at the Mark Twain on Wilcox. Room three-oh-three. Go pick him up."

She closed her phone and looked at Bosch. Worse than judgment, he saw disappointment and dismissal in her eyes now.

"I have to go," she said. "I'd stay away from airports, subways and the malls until we find that cesium."

She turned and left him there. Bosch was watching her walk away when his phone started to buzz again and he answered without taking his eyes off her. It was Joe Felton, the deputy coroner.

"Harry, I've been trying to reach you."

"What's up, Joe?"

"We just swung by Queen of Angels to make a pickup—some gangbanger they pulled the plug on after a shooting yesterday in Hollywood."

Bosch remembered the case Jerry Edgar had mentioned.

"Yeah?"

Bosch knew that the medical examiner

wouldn't have called to waste his time. There was a reason.

"So, we're here now and I go into the break room to grab some caffeine and I overhear a couple of paramedics talking about a pickup that they just made. They said they just brought in a guy and the ER evaluation was ARS and it just made me wonder if it could be connected with the guy up on the overlook. You know, since he was wearing the radiation alert rings."

Bosch calmed his voice.

"Joe, what is ARS?"

"Acute radiation syndrome. The medics said they didn't know what the guy had. He was burned and he was puking all over the place. They transported him and the ER doc said it was a pretty bad exposure, Harry. Now the medics are waiting to see if they're exposed."

Bosch started walking toward Rachel Walling.

"Where'd they find this guy?"

"I didn't ask but I assume it was somewhere in Hollywood if they brought him in here."

Bosch started picking up speed.

"Joe, I want you to hang up and get somebody from hospital security to watch this guy. I'm on my way."

Bosch clapped the phone closed and began running toward Rachel as fast as he could.

SIXTEEN

THE TRAFFIC ON THE HOLLYWOOD FREEWAY was all flowing into downtown at a slow crawl. Under the laws of traffic physics—that for every action there is an equal and opposite reaction—Harry Bosch had clear sailing on the northbound lanes out. Of course, this was aided by the siren and flashing lights on his car, making what little traffic there was in front of him move quickly to the side and out of the way. *Applied force* was another law Bosch knew well. He had the old Crown Vic up to ninety and his hands were white-knuckled on the wheel.

"Where are we going?" Rachel Walling yelled over the sound of the siren.

"I told you. I'm taking you to the cesium."

"What does that mean?"

"It means paramedics just brought a man with acute radiation syndrome into the emergency room at Queen of Angels. We'll be there in four minutes."

"Damn it! Why didn't you tell me?"

The answer was that he wanted a head start but he didn't tell her this. He remained silent while she opened her cell phone and punched in a number. She then reached up to the car's roof and flicked off the siren toggle.

"What are you doing?" Bosch exclaimed. "I need that to—"

"I need to be able to talk!"

Bosch took his foot off the accelerator and dropped it down to seventy to be safe. A moment later her call was connected and Bosch listened to her bark commands. He hoped it was at Brenner and not Maxwell.

"Divert the team from the Mark Twain to Queen of Angels. Scramble a contamination team and get them there, too. Send backup units and a DOE assessment team. We have an exposure case that may lead us to the missing materials. Do it and call me back. I'll be on-site in three minutes."

She closed the phone and Bosch hit the siren toggle.

"I said four minutes!" he yelled.

"Impress me!" she yelled back.

He pinned the accelerator again even though he didn't need to. He was confident they would be first to the hospital. They were already past Silver Lake on the freeway and closing in on Hollywood. But the truth was that any time he could legitimately hit ninety on the Hollywood Freeway he took advantage. There were not many in the city who could say they had done that during daylight hours.

"Who is the victim?" Rachel shouted.

"No idea."

They were silent for a long period. Bosch concentrated on the driving. And his thoughts. There were so many things that bothered him about the case. Soon he had to share them.

"How do you think they targeted him?" he said.

"What?" Walling replied, coming out of her own thoughts.

"Moby and El-Fayed. How'd they zero in on Stanley Kent?"

"I don't know. Maybe if this is one of them at the hospital, we'll get to ask."

Bosch let some time go by. He was tired of yelling. But then he called over another question.

"Doesn't it bother you that everything came out of that house?"

"What are you talking about?"

"The gun, the camera, the computer they used. Everything. There's Coke in liter bottles in the pantry and they tied Alicia Kent up with the same snap ties she uses to hold her roses up in the backyard. Doesn't that bother you? They had nothing but a knife and ski masks when they went through that door. Doesn't that bother you at all about this case?"

"You have to remember, these people are resourceful. They teach them that in the camps. El-Fayed was trained in an al Qaeda camp in Afghanistan. He in turn taught Nassar. They make do with what's available. You could say that they took down the World Trade Center with a couple of airliners or a couple of box cutters.

It's all in how you look at it. More important than what tools they have is their relentlessness—something I am sure you can appreciate."

Bosch was about to respond but they came up on the exit and he had to concentrate on weaving around the traffic on surface streets. In two minutes he finally killed the siren and pulled into the ambulance run at Queen of Angels.

Felton met them in the crowded emergency room and led the way to the treatment area, where there were six ER bays. A private security cop stood outside one of the curtained spaces and Bosch moved forward, showing his badge. After barely acknowledging the rent-a-cop he split the curtain and moved into the treatment bay.

Alone in the curtained space was the patient, a small, dark-haired man with brown skin lying beneath a spider web of tubes and wires extending from overhead medical machinery to his limbs, chest, mouth and nose. The hospital bed was encased in a clear, plastic tent. The man barely took up half the bed and somehow looked like a victim under attack by the apparatus around him.

His eyes were half-lidded and unmoving.

Most of his body was exposed. Some sort of modesty towel had been taped over his genitals but his legs and torso were visible. The right side of his stomach and right hip were covered with blooms of thermal burns. His right hand exhibited the same burns—painful-looking red rings surrounding purplish wet eruptions in the skin. A clear gel had been spread over the burns but it didn't look like it was helping.

"Where is everybody?" Bosch asked.

"Harry, don't get close," Walling warned. "He's not conscious so let's just back out and talk to the doctor before we do anything."

Bosch pointed to the patient's burns.

"Could this be from the cesium?" Bosch asked. "It can happen that fast?"

"From direct exposure in a concentrated amount, yeah. It depends on how long the exposure was. It looks like this guy was carrying the stuff in his pocket."

"Does he look like Moby or El-Fayed?"

"No, he doesn't look like either one of them. Come on."

She stepped back through the curtain and Bosch followed. She ordered the security man to get the ER doctor who was treating the man. She flipped open her phone and pushed a single button. Her call was answered quickly.

"This is legit," she said. "We have a direct exposure. We need to set up a command post and a containment protocol here."

She listened and then answered a question.

"No, neither one. I don't have an ID yet. I'll call it in as soon as I do."

She closed the phone and looked at Bosch.

"The radiation team will be here inside of ten minutes," she said. "I'll be directing the command post."

A woman in hospital blues walked up to them, carrying a clipboard.

"I'm Dr. Garner. You need to stay away from that patient until we know more about what happened to him."

Walling and Bosch showed her their credentials.

"What can you tell us?" Walling asked.

"Not much at this time. He's in full prodromal syndrome—the first symptoms of exposure. The trouble is, we don't know what he was exposed to or for how long. That gives us no gray count and without that we don't have a specific treatment protocol. We're winging it."

"What are the symptoms?" Walling asked.

"Well, you see the burns. Those are the least of our problems. The most serious damage is internal. His immune system is shutting down and he's aspirated most of the lining of his stomach. His GI tract is shot. We stabilized him but I'm not holding out a great deal of hope. The stress on the body pushed him into cardiac arrest. We just had the blue team in here fifteen minutes ago."

"How long is it between exposure and the start of this produro-whatever syndrome?" Bosch asked.

"Prodromal. It can happen within an hour of first exposure."

Bosch looked at the man beneath the plastic canopy enclosing the bed. He remembered the phrase Captain Hadley had used when Samir was dying on the floor of his prayer room. *He's circling the drain.* He knew the man on the hospital bed was circling it as well.

"What can you tell us about who he is and where he was found?" Bosch asked the doctor.

"You'll have to talk to the paramedics about where he was found," Garner answered. "I didn't have time to get into that. And all I heard was that he was found in the street. He had collapsed. And as far as who he is . . ."

She raised the clipboard and read from the top sheet.

"He's listed as Digoberto Gonzalves, age forty-one. There's no address here. That's all I know right now."

Walling stepped away, pulling her phone out again. Bosch knew she was going to call in the name, have it run through the terrorism databases.

"Where are his clothes?" he asked the doctor. "Where's his wallet?"

"His clothing and all his possessions were removed from the ER because of exposure concerns."

"Did anybody look through them?"

"No, sir, nobody was going to risk it."

"Where was it all taken?"

"You'll have to get that information from the nursing staff."

She pointed to a nursing station in the center of the treatment area. Bosch headed that way. The nurse at the desk told Bosch that everything from the patient was placed in a medical waste container that was then taken to the hospital's incinerator. It was not clear whether this was done in accordance with the hospital's protocol for dealing with contamination cases or out of utter fear of the unknown factors involved with Gonzalves.

"Where's the incinerator?"

Rather than give him directions, the nurse called over the security guard and told him to take Bosch to the incinerator room. Before Bosch could go, Walling called to him.

"Take this," she said, holding out the radiation-alert monitor she had taken off her belt. "And remember, we have a radiation team coming. Don't risk yourself. If that goes off, you back away. I mean it. *You back away.*"

"Got it."

Bosch put the alert monitor in his pocket. He and the guard quickly headed down a hallway and then took a stairway to the basement. They then took another hallway that seemed to run at least a block in length to the far side of the building.

When they got to the incinerator room the space was empty and there appeared to be no active burning of medical waste occurring. There was a three-foot canister on the floor.

Its top was sealed with tape that said CAU-TION: HAZARDOUS WASTE.

Bosch took out his key chain which had a small penknife on it. He squatted down next to the canister and cut the security tape. In his peripheral vision he noticed the security guard step back.

"Maybe you should wait outside," Bosch said. "There's no need for both of us to—"

He heard the door close behind him before he finished the sentence.

He looked down at the canister, took a breath and removed the top. Digoberto Gonzalves's clothes had been haphazardly dropped into the container.

Bosch took the monitor Walling had given him out of his pocket and waved it over the open canister like a magic wand. The monitor remained silent. He let his breath out. Then, as smoothly as emptying a wastepaper basket at home, he turned the canister upside down and dumped its contents onto the concrete floor. He rolled the canister aside and once again moved the monitor in a circular pattern over the clothes. There was no alarm.

Gonzalves's clothes had been cut off his body with scissors. There were a pair of dirty blue jeans, a work shirt, T-shirt, underwear and socks. There was a pair of work boots with the laces cut by the scissors as well. Lying loose on the floor in the middle of the clothing was a small, black leather wallet.

Bosch started with the clothing. In the pocket of the work shirt were a pen and a tire pressure gauge. He found work gloves sticking out of one of the rear pockets of the jeans and then removed a set of keys and a cell phone from the left front pocket. He thought about the burns he had seen on Gonzalves's right hip and hand. But when he opened the right front pocket of the jeans there was no cesium. The pocket was empty.

Bosch put the cell phone and keys down next to the wallet and studied what he had. On one of the keys Bosch saw a Toyota insignia. Now he knew that a vehicle was part of the equation. He opened the phone and tried to find the call directory but couldn't figure it out. He put it aside and opened the wallet.

There wasn't much. The wallet contained a Mexican driver's license with the name and photo of Digoberto Gonzalves. He was from Oaxaca. In one of the slots he found photos of a woman and three young children — shots that Bosch guessed were taken back in Mexico. There was no green card or citizenship document. There were no credit cards and in the billfold section there were only six dollar bills along with several tickets from pawnshops located in the Valley.

Bosch put the wallet down next to the phone, stood up and got out his own phone. He scrolled the directory until he found Walling's cell number.

She answered his call immediately.

"I checked his clothes. No cesium."

There was no response.

"Rachel, did you—"

"Yes, I heard. I just wish you had found it, Harry. I just wish this could be over."

"Me, too. Did anything come through on the name?"

"What name?"

"Gonzalves. You called it in, right?"

"Oh, right, yeah. No, nothing. And I mean nothing, not even a driver's license. I think it must be an alias."

"I've got a Mexican driver's license here. I think the guy's an illegal."

She gave that some thought before responding.

"Well, it's believed that Nassar and El-

Fayed came in across the Mexican border. Maybe that's the connection. Maybe this guy was working with them."

"I don't know, Rachel. I've got work clothes here. Work boots. I think this guy—"

"Harry, I've gotta go. My team is here."

"All right. I'm heading back up."

Bosch pocketed his phone, then gathered the clothing and boots and put them all back in the canister. He put the wallet, keys and cell phone on top of the clothing and took the canister with him. On the long walk back down the hallway to the stairs he pulled out his phone again and called the city's communications center. He asked the dispatcher to dig out the details on the paramedic call that had brought Gonzalves to Queen of Angels and was put on hold.

He got all the way up the steps and back to the ER before the dispatcher came back on the line.

"The call you asked about came in at ten-oh-five from a phone registered to Easy Print at nine-thirty Cahuenga Boulevard. Man down in the parking lot. Fire department paramedics responded from station fifty-four. Response time six minutes, nineteen seconds. Anything else?"

"What's the nearest cross at that location?"

After a moment the dispatcher told him the cross street was Lankershim Boulevard. Bosch thanked her and disconnected.

The address where Gonzalves collapsed was not far from the Mulholland overlook. Bosch realized that almost every location associated with the case so far—from the murder site to the victim's house to Ramin Samir's house and now to the spot where Gonzalves collapsed—could fit on one page of a Thomas Brothers map book. Murder cases in L.A. usually dragged him all over the map book. But this one wasn't roaming. It was staying close.

Bosch looked around the ER. He noticed that all the people who had been crowding the waiting room before were now gone. There had been an evacuation and agents in protective gear were moving about the area with radiation monitors. He spotted Rachel Walling by the nursing station and walked over to her. He held out the canister.

"Here's the guy's stuff."

She took the canister and put it down on the floor, then called over to one of the men in protection gear. She told him to take charge of the canister. She then looked back at Bosch.

"There's a cell phone in there," he told her. "They might be able to get something out of that."

"I'll tell them."

"How's the victim doing?"

"Victim?"

"Whether he's involved in this or not he is still a victim."

"If you say so. He's still out of it. I don't know if we'll ever get the chance to talk to him."

"Then I'm leaving."

"What? Where? I'm going with you."

"I thought you had to run the CP."

"I passed it off. If there's no cesium here I'm not staying. I'll stick with you. Let me just tell some people I'm leaving to follow a lead."

Bosch hesitated. But deep down he knew he wanted her with him.

"I'll be out front in the car."

"Where are we going?"

"I don't know if Digoberto Gonzalves is a terrorist or just a victim, but I do know one thing. He drives a Toyota. And I think I know where we'll find it."

SEVENTEEN

HARRY BOSCH KNEW that the physics of traffic would not work for him in the Cahuenga Pass. The Hollywood Freeway always moved slowly in both directions through the bottleneck created by the cut in the mountain chain. He decided to stay on surface streets and take Highland Avenue past the Hollywood Bowl and up into the pass. He filled Rachel Walling in along the way.

"The call for paramedics came from a print shop on Cahuenga near Lankershim. Gonzalves must have been in the area when he collapsed. The initial call said a man was down in the parking lot. I'm hoping that the Toyota he was driving is right there. I'm betting that if we find it, we find the cesium. The mystery is why he had it."

"And why he was foolish enough to put it in his pocket unprotected," Walling added.

"You're basing that on him knowing what he had. Maybe he didn't. Maybe this isn't what we think it is."

"There's got to be a connection, Bosch, between Gonzalves and Nassar and El-Fayed. He probably brought them across the border."

He almost smiled. He knew she had used his last name as a term of endearment. He remembered how she used to do that.

"And don't forget about Ramin Samir?" he said.

Walling shook her head.

"I'm still thinking he was a red herring," she said. "A misdirection."

"A good one," Bosch responded. "It took the mighty Captain Done Badly out of the picture."

She laughed.

"Is that what they call him?"

Bosch nodded.

"Not to his face, of course."

"And what do they call you? Something tough and hard-headed, I'm sure."

He glanced over at her and shrugged. He thought about telling her that his Vietnam nickname was Hari Kari but that would require further explanation and there wasn't the time right now and this wasn't the place.

He took the ramp up to Cahuenga from Highland. It ran parallel to the freeway and as soon as he checked he saw that he had been right. The traffic over on the freeway was frozen in both directions.

"You know, I still had your number in my cell's directory," he said. "I guess I never wanted to delete it."

"I was wondering about that when you left me that mean message today about the cigarette ash."

"I don't suppose you kept mine, Rachel."

She paused a long moment before answering.

"I think you're still on my phone, too, Harry."

This time he had to smile, even though he was back to being Harry with her. There's hope after all, he thought.

They were approaching Lankershim Boulevard. To the right it dropped down into a tunnel that went beneath the freeway. To the left it ended at a strip shopping center that included the Easy Print franchise from which the call to paramedics had originated. Bosch's eyes searched the vehicles in the small parking lot, looking for a Toyota.

He glided into the left-turn lane and waited to pull into the lot. He swiveled in his seat and checked the parking along both sides of Cahuenga. A quick glance showed no Toyotas but he knew that there were many different car models and pickup trucks in the brand. If they didn't find the car in the print shop lot, then they would have to work the curbside parking looking for it.

"Do you have a plate or any description?" Walling asked. "How about a color?"

"No, no and no."

Bosch remembered then that she had the habit of asking multiple questions at once.

He made the turn on yellow and pulled into the lot. There were no parking spaces available but he wasn't interested in parking. He cruised slowly, checking each car. There were no Toyotas.

"Where's a Toyota when you need one?"

he said. "It's got to be in this area somewhere."

"Maybe we should check the street," Walling suggested.

He nodded and nosed his car into the alley at the end of the parking lot. He was going to turn left to turn around and go back to
the street. But when he checked to see if he
was clear on the right he saw an old white
pickup truck with a camper shell parked half
a block down the alley next to a green trash
Dumpster. The truck was facing them and he
couldn't tell what the make of it was.

"Is that a Toyota?" he asked.

Walling turned and looked.

"Bosch, you're a genius," she exclaimed.

Bosch turned and drove toward the truck
and as he got closer he could see that it was
indeed a Toyota. So could Walling. She pulled
out her phone but Bosch reached across and
put his hand on it.

"Let's just check it out first. I could be
wrong about this."

"No, Bosch, you're on a roll."

But she put the phone away. Bosch pulled
slowly past the pickup, giving it a once-over.
He then turned around at the end of the block
and came back. He stopped his car ten feet

behind it. There was no plate on the back. A cardboard LOST TAG sign had been put in its place.

Bosch wished he had brought the keys he had found in Digoberto Gonzalves's pocket. They got out and approached the truck, coming up on either side of it. When he got close Bosch noticed that the rear window hatch of the camper shell had been left open a couple of inches. He reached forward and pulled it up all the way. An air-pressure hinge held it open. Bosch leaned in close to look into the interior. It was dark because the truck was parked in shadow and the windows on the shell were darkly tinted.

"Harry, you have that monitor?"

He pulled her radiation monitor out of his pocket and held it up in his hand as he leaned into the darkness of the truck's cargo hold. No alarm sounded. He leaned back out and put the monitor on his belt. He then reached in to the latch and lowered the truck's rear gate.

The back of the truck was piled with junk. There were empty bottles and cans strewn everywhere, a leather desk chair with a broken leg, scrap pieces of aluminum, an old water cooler and other debris. And there by the raised wheel well on the right side was a lead gray container that looked like a small mop bucket on wheels.

"There," he said. "Is that the pig?"

"I think it is," Walling said excitedly. "I think it is!"

There was no warning sticker on it or radiation-alert symbol. They had been peeled off. Bosch leaned into the truck and grabbed one of the handles. He pulled it clear of the debris around it and rolled it to the tailgate. The top was latched in four places.

"Do we open it and make sure the stuff is in there?" he asked.

"No," Walling said. "We back off and call in the team. They have protection."

She pulled her phone out again. While she called for the radiation team and backup units Bosch moved to the front of the truck. He looked through the window and into the cab. He saw a half-eaten breakfast burrito sitting on a flattened brown bag on the center console. And he saw more junk on the passenger side. His eyes held on a camera that was sitting on an old briefcase with a broken handle on the passenger seat. The camera didn't appear broken or dirty. It looked brand-new.

Bosch checked the door and found it un-

locked. He realized that Gonzalves had forgotten about his truck and his possessions
when the cesium started burning through his
body. He had gotten out and stumbled toward the parking lot, seeking help, leaving
everything else behind and unlocked.

Bosch opened the driver's door and
reached in with the radiation monitor. Nothing happened. No alert. He stood back up
and replaced it on his belt. From his pocket
he got out a pair of latex gloves and put them
on while listening to Walling talking to someone about finding the pig.

"No, we didn't open it," she said. "Do you
want us to?"

She listened some before responding.

"I didn't think so. Just get them here as
fast as you can and maybe this will all be
over."

Bosch leaned back into the truck through
the driver-side door and picked up the camera. It was a Nikon digital and he remembered that the lens cover found beneath the
master bed at the Kent house by the SID
team had said Nikon on it. He believed he
was holding the camera that had taken the
photograph of Alicia Kent. He turned it on
and for once he knew what he was doing as

he examined a piece of electronic equipment. He had a digital camera that he routinely carried with him when he went to Hong Kong to visit his daughter. He'd bought it when he had taken her to Disneyland China.

His camera wasn't a Nikon but he was able to quickly determine that the camera he had just found had no photos in its memory because the chip had been removed.

Bosch put the camera down and began looking through the things piled on the passenger seat. In addition to the broken briefcase, there was a child's lunch box as well as a manual for operating an Apple computer and a poker from a fireplace tool set. Nothing connected and nothing interested him. He noticed a golf putter and a rolled-up poster on the floor in front of the seat.

He moved the brown bag and the burrito out of the way and shifted his weight to one elbow on the armrest between the seats so he could reach over and open the glove compartment. And there, sitting in the otherwise empty space, was a handgun. Bosch lifted it out and turned it in his hand. It was a Smith & Wesson .22 caliber revolver.

"I think we've got the murder weapon here," he called out.

There was no response from Walling. She was still at the back of the truck talking on her phone, still issuing orders in an animated voice.

Bosch returned the weapon to the glove box and closed it, deciding to leave the weapon in its place for the Forensics team. He noticed the rolled-up poster again and decided for no reason other than curiosity to take a look at it. Using his elbow on the center armrest for support he unrolled it across all of the junk on the passenger seat. It was a chart depicting twelve yoga positions.

Bosch immediately thought about the discolored space he had seen on the wall in the workout room at the Kent house. He wasn't sure but he thought the dimensions of the poster would be a close match to that space on the wall. He quickly rerolled the poster and started to back out of the cab so he could show Walling the discovery.

But as he was pulling out he noticed that the armrest between the seats was also a storage compartment. He stopped and opened it.

He froze. There was a cup holder and in it were several steel capsules resembling bullet cartridges closed flat on both ends.

The steel was so polished it almost looked like silver. It might even have been mistaken for silver.

Bosch moved the radiation monitor over the capsules in a circular pattern. There was no alarm. He turned the device over in his hand and looked at it. He saw a small switch on its side. With his thumb he pushed it up. A blaring alarm suddenly went off, the frequency of tones so fast that they sounded like one long, eardrum-piercing siren.

Bosch jumped back out of the truck and slammed the door shut. The poster fell to the ground.

"Harry!" Walling yelled. "What?"

She rushed toward him, closing her phone on her hip. Bosch pushed the switch again and turned the monitor off.

"What is it?" she yelled.

Bosch pointed toward the truck's door.

"The gun's in the glove box and the cesium's in the center compartment."

"What?"

"The cesium is in the compartment under the armrest. He took the capsules out of the pig. That's why they weren't in his pocket. They were in the center armrest."

He touched his right hip, the place where

Gonzalves was burned by radiation. The same spot would have been next to the armrest compartment when he was sitting in the truck.

Rachel didn't say anything for a long moment. She just stared at his face.

"Are you okay?" she finally asked.

Bosch almost laughed.

"I don't know," he said. "Ask me in about ten years."

She hesitated as if she knew something but couldn't share it.

"What?" Bosch asked.

"Nothing. You should be checked out, though."

"What are they going to be able to do? Look, I wasn't in the truck that long. It's not like Gonzalves, who was sitting in there with it. He was practically eating off of it."

She didn't answer. Bosch handed her the monitor.

"It was never on. I thought it was on when you gave it to me."

She took it and looked at it in her hand.

"I thought it was, too."

Bosch thought about how he had carried the monitor in his pocket rather than clipped to his belt. He had probably switched it off unknowingly when he had twice put it in and removed it. He looked back at the truck and wondered if he had possibly just hurt or killed himself.

"I need a drink of water," he said. "I've got a bottle in the trunk."

Bosch walked back to the rear of his car. Using the open trunk lid to shield Walling's view of him, he leaned his hands down on the bumper for support and tried to decipher the messages his body was sending to his brain. He felt something happening but didn't know if it was something physiological or if the shakes he felt were just an emotional response to what had just happened. He remembered what the ER doctor had said about Gonzalves and how the most serious damage was internal. Was his own immune system shutting down? Was he circling the drain?

He suddenly thought of his daughter, getting a vision of her at the airport the last time he saw her.

He cursed out loud.

"Harry?"

Bosch looked around the trunk lid. Rachel was walking toward him.

"The teams are headed this way. They'll be here in five minutes. How do you feel?"

"I think I'm okay."

"Good. I talked to the head of the team. He thinks the exposure was too short to be anything serious. But you still should go to the ER and get checked out."

"We'll see."

He reached into the trunk and got a liter bottle of water out of his kit. It was an emergency bottle he kept for surveillances that dragged on longer than expected. He opened it and took two strong pulls. The water wasn't cold but it felt good going down. His throat was dry.

Bosch recapped the bottle and put it back in the kit. He stepped around the car to Walling. As he walked toward her he looked past her to the south. He realized that the alley they were in extended several blocks past the back of the Easy Print and ran behind all the storefronts and offices on Cahuenga. All the way down to Barham.

In the alley every twenty yards or so was a green Dumpster positioned perpendicular to the rear of the structures. Bosch realized they had been pushed out of spaces between the buildings and fenced corrals. Just like in Silver Lake, it was pickup day and the Dumpsters were waiting for the city trucks to come.

Suddenly it all came to him. Like fusion. Two elements coming together and creating something new. The thing that bothered him about the crime scene photos, the yoga poster, everything. The gamma rays had shot right through him but they had left him enlightened. He knew. He understood.

"He's a scavenger."

"Who is?"

"Digoberto Gonzalves," Bosch said, his eyes looking down the alley. "It's collection day. The Dumpsters are all pushed out for the city trucks. Gonzalves is a scavenger, a Dumpster diver, and he knew they would be out and this would be a good time to come here."

He looked at Walling before completing the thought.

"And so did somebody else," he said.

"You mean he found the cesium in a Dumpster?"

Bosch nodded and pointed down the alley.

"All the way at the end, that's Barham. Barham takes you up to Lake Hollywood. Lake Hollywood takes you to the overlook. This case never leaves the map page."

Walling came over and stood in front of him, blocking his view. Bosch could now hear sirens in the distance.

"What are you saying? That Nassar and El-Fayed took the cesium and stashed it in a Dumpster at the bottom of the hill? Then this scavenger comes along and finds it?"

"I'm saying you've got the cesium back so now we're looking at this as a homicide again. You come down from the overlook and you can be in this alley in five minutes."

"So what? They stole the cesium and killed Kent just so they could come down here and stash it? Is that what you're saying? Or are you saying they just threw it all away? Why would they do that? I mean, does that make any sense at all? I mean, I don't see that scaring people in the way we know they want to scare us."

Bosch noted that she had asked six questions at once this time, possibly a new record.

"Nassar and El-Fayed were never near the cesium," he said. "That's what I'm saying."

He walked over to the truck and picked the

rolled poster up off the ground. He handed it to Rachel. The sirens were getting louder.

She unrolled the poster in her hands and looked at it.

"What is this? What does it mean?"

Bosch took it back from her and started rolling it up.

"Gonzalves found that in the same Dumpster where he found the gun and the camera and the lead pig."

"So? What does it *mean,* Harry?"

Two fed cars pulled into the alley a block away and started making their way toward them, weaving around the Dumpsters pushed out for pickup. As they got close Bosch could see that the driver of the lead car was Jack Brenner.

"Do you hear me, Harry? What does it—"

Bosch's knees suddenly seemed to give out and he fell into her, throwing his arms around her to stop himself from hitting the ground.

"Bosch!"

She grabbed on and held him.

"Uh . . . I'm not feeling so good," he mumbled. "I think I better . . . can you take me to my car?"

She helped him straighten up and then

started walking him toward his car. He put his arm over her shoulders. Car doors were slamming behind them as the agents got out.

"Where are the keys?" Walling asked.

He held the key ring out to her just as Brenner ran up to them.

"What is it? What's wrong?"

"He was exposed. The cesium is in the center console in the truck cab. Be careful. I'm going to take him to the hospital."

Brenner stepped back, as if whatever Bosch had were contagious.

"Okay," he said. "Call me when you can."

Bosch and Walling kept moving toward the car.

"Come on, Bosch," Walling said. "Stay with me. Hang in there and we'll get you taken care of."

She had called him by his last name again.

EIGHTEEN

THE CAR JERKED FORWARD as Walling pulled out of the alley and into southbound traffic on Cahuenga.

"I'm taking you back to Queen of Angels so Dr. Garner can take a look at you," she said. "Just hang in there for me, Bosch."

He knew it was likely that the last-name endearments were about to come to an end. He pointed toward the left-turn lane that led onto Barham Boulevard.

"Never mind the hospital," he said. "Take me back to the Kent house."

"What?"

"I'll get checked out later. Go to the Kent house. Here's the turn. Go!"

She slipped into the left-turn lane.

"What's going on?"

"I'm fine. I'm okay."

"What are you telling me, that that little fainting spell back there was—"

"I had to get you away from the crime scene and away from Brenner so I could check this out and talk to you. Alone."

"Check what out? Talk about what? Do you realize what you just did? I thought I was saving your life. Now Brenner or one of those other guys will take the credit for the recovery of the cesium. Thanks a lot, asshole. That was my crime scene."

He opened his jacket and pulled out the rolled-up and folded yoga poster.

"Don't worry about it," he said. "You can get the credit for the arrests. You just might not want it."

He opened the poster, letting the top half flop over his knees. He was only interested in the bottom half.

"Dhanurasana," he said.

Walling glanced over at him and then down at the poster.

"Would you start telling me what's going on?"

"Alicia Kent practices yoga. I saw the mats in the workout room at the house."

"I saw them, too. So what?"

"Did you see the sun discoloration on the wall where a picture or a calendar or maybe a poster had been taken down?"

"Yes, I saw it."

Bosch held up the poster.

"I'm betting that we go in there and this will be a perfect fit. This is a poster Gonzalves found with the cesium."

"And what will that mean?—if it's a perfect fit."

"It will mean that it was almost a perfect crime. Alicia Kent conspired to kill her husband and, if it hadn't been for Digoberto Gonzalves just happening to find the tossed-out evidence, she would have gotten away with it."

Walling shook her head dismissively.

"Come on, Harry. Are you saying she conspired with international terrorists to kill her husband in exchange for the cesium? I can't believe I am even doing this. I need to get back to the crime scene."

She started checking her mirrors, getting

ready to make a U-turn. They were going up Lake Hollywood Drive now and would be at the house in two minutes.

"No, keep going. We're almost there. Alicia Kent conspired with someone but it wasn't a terrorist. The cesium being dumped in the trash proves that. You said it yourself, there is no way that Moby and El-Fayed would steal this stuff to just dump it. So what does that tell you? This *wasn't* a heist. It actually *was* a murder. The cesium was just a red herring. Just like Ramin Samir. And Moby and El-Fayed? They were part of the misdirection as well. This poster will help prove it."

"How?"

"Dhanurasana, the rocking bow."

He held the poster up and over so she could glance at the yoga pose depicted in the bottom corner. It showed a woman with her arms behind her back, holding her ankles and creating a bow with the front of her body. She looked like she was hog-tied.

Walling glanced back at the curving road and then took another long look at the poster and the pose.

"We go into the house and see if this fits that space on the wall," Bosch said. "If it fits, that means she and the killer took it off the wall because they didn't want to risk that we might see it and connect it with what happened to her."

"It's a stretch, Harry. A huge one."

"Not when you put it in context."

"Which you, of course, can do."

"As soon as we get to the house."

"Hope you still have a key."

"You bet I do."

Walling turned onto Arrowhead Drive and punched the accelerator. But after a block she took her foot off, slowed down and shook her head again.

"This is ridiculous. She gave us the name Moby. There is no way she could have known he was in this country. And then up on the overlook, your own witness said that the shooter called out to Allah as he pulled the trigger. How can—"

"Let's just try the poster on the wall. If it fits, I'll lay the whole thing out for you. I promise. If it doesn't fit, then I will quit—bothering you with it."

She relented and drove the remaining block to the Kent house without another word. There was no longer a bureau car sitting out front. Bosch guessed that it was all hands on deck at the cesium recovery scene.

"Thank God I don't have to deal with Maxwell again," he said.

Walling didn't even smile.

Bosch got out with the poster and his file containing the crime scene photos. He used Stanley Kent's keys to open the front door and they proceeded to the workout room. They took positions on either side of the rectangular sun-discoloration mark and Bosch unrolled the poster. They each took a side and held the top corner of the poster to the top corner of the mark. Bosch put his other hand on the center of the poster and flattened it against the wall. The poster was a perfect fit over the mark on the wall. What was more was that the tape marks on the wall matched up with tape marks and old tape on the poster. To Bosch there was no doubt. The poster found by Digoberto Gonzalves in a Dumpster off Cahuenga had definitely come from Alicia Kent's home yoga studio.

Rachel let go of her side of the poster and headed out of the room.

"I'll be in the living room. I can't wait to hear you put this together."

Bosch rolled the poster up and followed. Walling took a seat in the same chair Bosch had put Maxwell in a few hours earlier. He remained standing in front of her.

"The fear was that the poster could be a tip-off," he said. "Some smart agent or detective would see the rocking-bow pose and start thinking, This woman does yoga, maybe she could handle being hog-tied like that, maybe it was her idea, maybe she did it to help sell the misdirection. So they couldn't take the chance. The poster had to go. It went into the Dumpster with the cesium, the gun and everything else they used. Except for the ski masks and the phony map they planted with the car at Ramin Samir's house."

"She's a master criminal," Walling said sarcastically.

Bosch was undeterred. He knew he'd convince her.

"If you get your people out there to check that line of Dumpsters, you'll find the rest—the Coke-bottle silencer, the gloves, the first set of snap ties, every—"

"The first set of snap ties?"

"That's right. I'll get to that."

Walling remained unimpressed.

"You better get to a lot of it. Because there are big gaps in this thing, man. What about

the name Moby? What about the citing of Allah by the shooter? What—"

Bosch held up a hand.

"Just hold on," he said. "I need some water. My throat is raw from all of this talking."

He went into the kitchen, remembering
that he saw bottles of chilled water in the refrigerator while searching the kitchen earlier
in the day.

"You want anything?" he called out.

"No," she called back. "It's not our house,
remember?"

He opened the refrigerator, took out a bottle of water and drank half of it while standing
in front of the open door. The cool air felt
good, too. He closed the door but then immediately reopened it. He had seen something. On the top shelf was a plastic bottle of
grape juice. He took it out and looked at it,
remembering that when he went through the
trash bag in the garage he had found paper
towels with grape juice on them.

Another piece of the puzzle fell into place.
He put the bottle back in the refrigerator and
then returned to the living room, where Rachel was waiting for the story. Once again,
he remained standing.

"Okay, when was it that you captured the terrorist known as Moby on video at the port?"

"What does—"

"Please, just answer the question."

"August twelfth last year."

"Okay, August twelfth. Then what, some sort of alert went out through the bureau and all of Homeland Security?"

She nodded.

"Not for a while, though," she said. "It took almost two months of video analysis to confirm it was Nassar and El-Fayed. I wrote the bulletin. It went out October ninth as a confirmed domestic sighting."

"Out of curiosity, why didn't you go public with it?"

"Because we have—actually, I can't tell you."

"You just did. You must have someone or someplace where you think these two might show up under surveillance. If you go public, they might just go underground and never show up again."

"Can we go back to your story, please?"

"Fine. So the bulletin went out October ninth. That was the day the plan to kill Stanley Kent began."

Walling folded her arms across her chest and just stared at him. Bosch thought that maybe she was beginning to see where he was going with the story and she didn't like it.

"It works best if you start from the end and go backwards," Bosch said. "Alicia Kent gave you the name Moby. How could she have gotten that name?"

"She overheard one of them calling the other one by that name."

Bosch shook his head.

"No, she told you she overheard it. But if she was lying, how would she know the name to lie about it? Just coincidence that she gives the nickname of a guy who less than six months ago was confirmed as being in the country—in L.A. County, no less? I don't think so, Rachel, and neither do you. The odds of that probably can't be calculated."

"Okay, so you're saying that somebody in the bureau or another agency that received the FBI bulletin I wrote gave her the name."

Bosch nodded and pointed at her.

"Right. He gave her the name so she could come out with it while being questioned by the FBI's master interrogator. That name along with the plan to dump the car in front of

Ramin Samir's house would act in concert to send this whole thing down the wrong road with the FBI and everybody else chasing after terrorists who had nothing to do with it."

"He?"

"I'm getting to that now. You are right, anybody who got a look at that bulletin would have been able to give her that name. My guess is that would be a lot of people. A lot of people just in L.A. alone. So how would we narrow it down to one?"

"You tell me."

Bosch opened the bottle and drank the rest of the water. He held the empty bottle in his hand as he continued.

"You narrow it down by continuing to go backwards. Where would Alicia Kent's life have intersected with one of those people in the agencies who knew about Moby?"

Walling frowned and shook her head.

"That could have been anywhere with those kinds of parameters. In line at the supermarket, or when she was buying fertilizer for her roses. Anywhere."

Bosch now had her right where he wanted her to be.

"Then narrow the parameters," he said. "Where would she have intersected with someone who knew about Moby but also knew that her husband had access to the sort of radioactive materials Moby might be interested in?"

Now she shook her head in a dismissive way.

"Nowhere. It would take a monumental co-incidence to—"

She stopped when it came to her. Enlightenment. And shock as she fully understood where Bosch was going.

"My partner and I visited the Kents to warn them early last year. I guess what you're saying is that that makes me a suspect."

Bosch shook his head.

"I said 'he,' remember? You didn't come here alone."

Her eyes fired when she registered the implication.

"That's ridiculous. There's no way. I can't believe you would . . ."

She didn't finish as her mind snagged on something, some memory that undermined her trust and loyalty to her partner. Bosch picked up on the tell and moved in closer.

"What?" he asked.

"Nothing."

"What?"

"Look," she insisted, "take my advice and tell no one this theory of yours. You're lucky you told me first. Because this makes you sound like some kind of crackpot with a vendetta. You have no evidence, no motive, no incriminating statements, nothing. You just have this thing you've spun out of . . . out of a yoga poster."

"There is no other explanation that fits with the facts. And I'm talking about the facts of the case. Not the fact that the bureau and Homeland Security and the rest of the federal government would love this to be a terrorism event so they can justify their existence and deflect criticism from other failings. Contrary to what you want to think, there *is* evidence and there *are* incriminating statements. If we put Alicia Kent on a lie detector, you'll find out that everything she told me, you and the master interrogator downtown is a lie. The real master was Alicia Kent. As in master manipulator."

Walling leaned forward and looked down at the floor.

"Thank you, Harry. That master interrogator you love deriding happens to have been me."

Bosch's mouth dropped open for a moment before he spoke.

"Oh . . . well . . . then, sorry . . . but it doesn't matter. The point is, she is a master liar. She lied about everything and now that we know the story, it will be easy to smoke her out."

Walling got up from her seat and walked over to the front picture window. The vertical blinds were closed but she split them with a finger and stared out into the street. Bosch could see her working the story over, grinding it down.

"What about the witness?" she asked without turning around. "He heard the shooter yell *Allah.* Are you saying he's part of this? Or are you saying they just happened to know he was there and yelled *Allah* as part of this master manipulation?"

Bosch gently tried to clear his throat. It was burning and making it difficult for him to talk.

"No, on that I think it's just a lesson in hearing what you want to hear. I plead guilty to not being much of a master interrogator myself. The kid told me that he heard the shooter yell it as he pulled the trigger. He said he wasn't sure but that it sounded like *Allah* and that, of course, worked with what I was thinking at the time. I heard what I wanted to hear."

Walling came away from the window, sat back down and folded her arms. Bosch finally sat down on a chair directly across from her. He continued.

"But how would the witness know it was the shooter and not the victim who yelled?" he asked. "He was more than fifty yards away. It was dark. How would he know that it wasn't Stanley Kent yelling out his last word before execution? The name of the woman he loved, because he was about to die not even knowing that she'd betrayed him."

"Alicia."

"Exactly. *Alicia* interrupted by a gunshot becomes *Allah*."

Walling relaxed her arms and leaned forward. As body language went, it was a good sign. It told Bosch he was pushing through.

"You said the *first* set of snap ties before," she said. "What were you talking about?"

Bosch nodded and handed across the file containing the crime scene photos. He had saved the best for last.

"Look at the photos," he said. "What do you see?"

She opened the file and started looking at the crime scene photos. They depicted the master bedroom in the Kent house from all angles.

"It's the master bedroom," she said. "What am I missing?"

"Exactly."

"What?"

"It's what you don't see. There are no clothes in the shot. She told us they told her to sit on the bed and take off her clothes. What are we supposed to believe, that they let her put the clothes away before they hogtied her? They let her put them in the hamper? Look at the last shot. It's the e-mail photo Stanley Kent got."

Walling looked through the file until she found the printout of the e-mail photo. She stared intently at it. He saw recognition break in her eyes.

"Now what do you see?"

"The robe," she said excitedly. "When we let her get dressed, she went to the *closet* to get her robe. There was no robe on that lounge chair!"

Bosch nodded and they started trading pieces of the story back and forth.

"What does that tell us?" he asked. "That

these considerate terrorists hung the robe up in the closet for her after taking the photo?"

"Or that maybe Mrs. Kent was tied up twice and the robe was moved in between?"

"And look again at the picture. The clock on the bed table is unplugged."

"Why?"

"I don't know but maybe they didn't want to worry about having any sort of time stamp on the photo. Maybe the first photo wasn't even taken yesterday. Maybe it came from a dry run two days ago or even two weeks."

Rachel nodded and Bosch knew she was committed. She was a believer.

"She was tied up once for the photo and then once again for the rescue," she said.

"Exactly. And that left her free to help carry out the plan on the overlook. She didn't kill her husband but she was up there in the other car. And once Stanley was dead and the cesium was dumped and the car was ditched at Samir's she and her partner came back home and she was tied up all over again."

"She wasn't passed out when we got there. That was an act and part of the plan. And her wetting the bed was a nice little touch to help sell it to us."

"The smell of urine also covered up the smell of grape juice."

"What do you mean?"

"The purple bruises on her wrists and ankles. Now we know she wasn't tied up for hours. But she still had those bruises. There's an opened bottle of grape juice in the fridge and paper towels soaked with it out in the trash can. She used grape juice to create the bruises."

"Oh, my God, I can't believe this."

"What?"

"When I was in the room with her at TIU. That small space. I thought I smelled grape in the room. I thought somebody had been in there before us and had been drinking grape juice. I smelled it!"

"There you go."

There was no doubt now. Bosch had her. But then a shadow of concern and doubt moved across Walling's face like a summer cloud.

"What about motive?" she asked. "This is a federal agent we're talking about. To move on this we need everything, even motive. There can be nothing left open to chance."

Bosch had been ready for the question.

"You saw the motive. Alicia Kent is a beautiful woman. Jack Brenner wanted her and Stanley Kent was in the way of that."

Walling's eyes widened in shock. Bosch pressed on with his case.

"That's the motive, Rachel. You—"

"But he—"

"Let me just finish. It goes like this. You and your partner show up here that day last year to give the Kents the warning about his occupation. Some kind of vibe is exchanged between Alicia and Jack. He gets interested, she gets interested. They meet on the sly for coffee or for drinks or whatever. One thing leads to another. An affair begins and it lasts and then it lasts to the point that it's time to start thinking about doing something. Leaving the husband. Or getting rid of him because there's insurance and half a company at stake. That's enough motive right there, Rachel, and that's what this case is about. It's not about cesium or terrorism or anything else. It's the basic equation: sex plus money equals murder. That's all."

She frowned and shook her head.

"You don't know what you are talking about. Jack Brenner is married and has three children. He's stable, boring and not interested. He wasn't—"

"Every man is interested. It doesn't matter if they're married or how many kids they have."

She spoke quietly.

"Would you listen and let me finish now? You are wrong about Brenner. He never met Alicia Kent before today. He wasn't my partner when I came here last year and I never told you he was."

Bosch was jolted by the news. He'd assumed that her current partner had been her partner last year. He'd had Brenner's image locked and loaded in his mind as he had unfolded the story.

"At the start of the year all partners in TIU were shuffled. It's the routine. It promotes a better team concept. I've been with Jack since January."

"Who was your partner last year, Rachel?"

She held his eyes for a long moment.

"It was Cliff Maxwell."

NINETEEN

HARRY BOSCH ALMOST LAUGHED but was too shocked to do anything but shake his head. Rachel Walling was telling him that Cliff Maxwell was Alicia Kent's partner in murder.

"I can't believe this," he finally said. "About five hours ago I had the killer handcuffed on the floor right here!"

Rachel looked mortified by the realization that the murder of Stanley Kent was an inside job and the theft of the cesium was nothing more than a well-played misdirection.

"You see the rest now?" Bosch asked. "You see how he would work it? Her husband's dead and he starts coming around out of sympathy and because he's on the case. They start dating, fall in love and nobody ever raises an eyebrow about it. They're still out there looking for Moby and El-Fayed."

"And what if we ever catch those guys?" Walling said, taking up the story. "They could deny being a part of this thing until Osama bin Laden dies in a cave of old age but who would believe them or care? There's nothing more ingenious than framing terrorists with a crime they didn't commit. They can never defend themselves."

Bosch nodded.

"A perfect crime," he said. "The only reason it blew up was because Digoberto Gonzalves checked that Dumpster. Without him we'd still be chasing Moby and El-Fayed, probably thinking that they had used Samir's place as a safe house."

"So, what do we do now, Bosch?"

Bosch shrugged but then answered anyway.

"I say we set up a classic rattrap. Put them both in rooms, ring the bell and say the first one who talks gets the deal. I'd bet on Alicia. She'll break and give him up, probably blame him for everything, say she was acting under his influence and control."

"Something tells me you're right. And the truth is, I don't think Maxwell was smart enough to pull this off. I worked with—"

Her cell phone started buzzing. She took it out of her pocket and looked at the screen.

"It's Jack."

"Find out where Maxwell is."

She answered the call and first replied to a few questions about Bosch's status, telling Brenner that he was okay but was losing his voice because his throat hurt. Bosch got up for another bottle of water but listened from the kitchen. Walling casually steered the call toward Maxwell.

"Hey, where's Cliff, by the way? I wanted to talk to him about that thing with Bosch in the hallway. I didn't like what he—"

She stopped and listened to the answer and Bosch saw her eyes immediately become alert. Something was wrong.

"When was that?" she asked.

She listened again and stood up.

"Listen, Jack, I've got to go. I think Bosch is about to be discharged. I'll check in as soon as I'm clear here."

She closed the phone and looked at Bosch.

"I can't stand lying to him. He won't forget it."

"What did he say?"

"He said there were too many agents at the recovery scene—just about everybody came out from downtown and they were standing around waiting on the radiation team. So Maxwell volunteered to go pick up the witness at the Mark Twain. Nobody had gotten around to it because I'd pulled off the original pickup team."

"He went alone?"

"That's what Jack said."

"How long ago?"

"A half hour."

"He's going to kill him."

Bosch started moving quickly toward the door.

TWENTY

BOSCH DROVE THIS TIME. On the way toward Hollywood he told Walling that Jesse Mitford had no phone in his room. The Mark Twain wasn't much when it came to full service. Instead, Bosch called the watch commander at Hollywood Division and asked him to send a patrol car to the hotel to check on the witness. He then called information and was connected to the front desk at the Mark Twain.

"Alvin, this is Detective Bosch. From this morning?"

"Yeah, yeah. What's up with you, Detective?"

"Has anyone come in asking for Stephen King?"

"Mmm, nope."

"In the last twenty minutes have you buzzed in anybody who looked like a cop or who wasn't a tenant there?"

"No, Detective. What's going on?"

"Listen, I need you to go up to that room and tell Stephen King to get out of there and then to call me on my cell."

"I got nobody to watch the desk, Detective."

"It's an emergency, Alvin. I need to get him out of there. It will take you less than five minutes. Here, write this down. My number is three-two-three, two-four-four, five-six-three-one. You got it?"

"I got it."

"Okay, go. And if anybody but me comes in there looking for him, say he checked out, took a refund and left. Go, Alvin, and thanks."

Bosch closed the phone and looked over at Rachel. His face showed his lack of confidence in the deskman.

"I think the guy's a tweaker."

Bosch increased his speed and tried to

concentrate on driving. They had just turned south on Cahuenga off Barham. He was thinking that, depending on traffic in Hollywood, they could get to the Mark Twain in another five minutes. This conclusion made him shake his head. With a half-hour lead Maxwell should already be at the Mark Twain. He wondered if he had slipped in the back way and already gotten to Mitford.

"Maxwell may have already gone in through the back," he told Walling. "I'm going to come in from the alley."

"You know," Walling said, "maybe he's not going to hurt him. He'll pick him up and talk to him, judge for himself if he saw enough at the overlook that he'd be a threat."

Bosch shook his head.

"No way. Maxwell's got to know that once the cesium was found, his plan was going down the toilet. He's got to take action against all threats. First the witness, then Alicia Kent."

"Alicia Kent? You think he'd make a move against her? This whole thing is because of her."

"Doesn't matter now. Survival instincts take over now and she's a threat. It goes with the territory. You cross the big line to be with her. You cross it again to save your—"

Bosch stopped talking as a sudden realization thudded in his chest. He cursed out loud and pinned the accelerator as they came out of the Cahuenga Pass. He cut across three lanes of Highland Avenue in front of the Hollywood Bowl and made a screeching U-turn in front of oncoming traffic. He punched it, and the car fishtailed wildly as he headed toward the southbound entrance to the Hollywood Freeway. Rachel grabbed the dashboard and a door handle to hold on.

"Harry, what are you doing? This is the wrong way!"

He flicked on the siren and the blue lights that flashed in the front grille and back window of the car. He yelled his response to Walling.

"Mitford is a misdirection. This is the right way. Who is the greater threat to Maxwell?"

"Alicia?"

"You bet and now's the best shot he has of getting her out of Tactical. Everybody's up in that alley with the cesium."

The freeway was moving pretty well and

the siren helped open it up further. Bosch figured Maxwell could have already gotten to downtown, depending on what kind of traffic he encountered.

Rachel opened her phone and started punching in numbers. She tried number after number but no one was answering.

"I can't get anybody," she yelled.

"Where's TIU?"

Walling didn't hesitate.

"On Broadway. You know where the Million Dollar Theater is? Same building. Entrance on Third."

Bosch flicked off the siren and opened his phone. He called his partner and Ferras answered right away.

"Ignacio, where are you?"

"Just got back to the office. Forensics worked the car for—"

"Listen to me. Drop what you're doing and meet me at the Third Street entrance to the Million Dollar Theater building. You know where that is?"

"What's going on?"

"Do you know where the Million Dollar Theater is?"

"Yeah, I know where it is."

"Meet me there at the Third Street entrance. I'll explain when I get there."

He closed the phone and hit the siren
again.

TWENTY-ONE

THE NEXT TEN MINUTES took ten hours. Bosch moved in and out of traffic and finally reached the Broadway exit in downtown. He killed the siren as he made the turn and headed down the hill toward their destination. They were three blocks away.

The Million Dollar Theater was built in a time when the movie business showed itself off in magnificent theater palaces that lined Broadway downtown. But it had been decades since a first-run film had been projected on a screen there. Its ornate façade had been covered by a lighted marquee that for a time announced religious revivals in-

stead of movies. Now the theater waited un-
used for renovation and redemption while
above it a once-grand office building was
twelve stories of midgrade office space and
residential lofts.

"Good place for a secret unit to have a secret office," Bosch said as the building came
into sight. "Nobody would've guessed."

Walling didn't respond. She was trying to
make another call. She then slapped the
phone closed in frustration.

"I can't even get our secretary. She always
takes lunch after one so there will be somebody in the office when the agents go to
lunch earlier."

"Where exactly is the squad and where
would Alicia Kent be in there?"

"We have the whole seventh floor. There's
a lounge room with a couch and a TV. They
put her in there so she could watch TV."

"How many in the squad?"

"Eight agents, the secretary and an office
manager. The office manager just went out
on maternity leave and the secretary must
be at lunch. I hope. But they wouldn't have
left Alicia Kent alone. It's against policy.
Somebody had to have stayed there with
her."

Bosch turned right on Third and immediately pulled to the curb. Ignacio Ferras was already there, leaning casually against his Volvo station wagon. In front of it was another parked car. A federal cruiser. Bosch and Walling got out. Bosch approached Ferras, and Walling went to look inside the fed car.

"Have you seen Maxwell?" Bosch asked.

"Who?"

"Agent Maxwell. The guy we put on the floor at the Kent house this morning."

"No, I haven't seen anybody. What—"

"It's his car," Walling said as she joined them.

"Ignacio, this is Agent Walling."

"Call me Iggy."

"Rachel."

They shook hands.

"Okay, then he's gotta be up there," Bosch said. "How many stairwells?"

"Three," Walling said. "But he'll use the one that comes out by his car."

She pointed to a pair of double steel doors near the corner of the building. Bosch headed over that way to see if they were locked. Ferras and Walling followed.

"What is going on?" Ferras asked.

"Maxwell is our shooter," Bosch said. "He is up—"

"What?"

Bosch checked the exit doors. There was no outside handle or knob. He turned to Ferras.

"Look, there's not a lot of time. Trust me, Maxwell is our guy and he's in this building to take out Alicia Kent. We're—"

"What is she doing here?"

"The FBI has a location here. She's here. No more questions, okay? Just listen. Agent Walling and I are going up in the elevator. I want you out here by this door. If Maxwell comes out, you take him down. You understand? You take him down."

"Got it."

"Good. Call for backup. We're going up."

Bosch reached over and tapped Ferras on the cheek.

"And stay frosty."

They left Ferras there and headed through the building's main entrance. There was no lobby to speak of, just an elevator. It opened at the push of the button and Walling used a key card to engage the seven button. They started going up.

"Something tells me you're never going to call him Iggy," Walling said.

Bosch ignored the comment but thought of something to ask.

"Does this thing have a bell or a tone that sounds when it reaches the floor?"

"I can't remem—I think it does ... yes, definitely."

"Great. We'll be sitting ducks."

Bosch pulled his Kimber out of its holster and chambered a round. Walling did the same with her weapon. Bosch pushed Walling to one side of the elevator while he took the other. He raised his gun. The elevator finally reached seven and there was a soft bell tone from outside. The door began to slide open, exposing Bosch first.

No one was there.

Rachel pointed to the left, signaling that the offices were to the left after they exited the elevator. Bosch lowered himself into a combat crouch and stepped out, his gun up and ready.

Again, no one was there.

He started moving to his left. Rachel came out and moved with him on his right flank. They came to a loft-style office with two rows of cubicles—the squad room—and three

private rooms that had been built free-stand-
ing in the open floor plan. There were large
racks of electronic equipment between the
cubicles, and every desk had two computer
screens on it. It looked like the whole place
could be packed up and moved at a moment's
notice.

Bosch stepped farther in, and through the
window in one of the private offices he saw a
man sitting in a chair, his head back and eyes
open. He looked like he was wearing a red
bib. But Bosch knew it was blood. The man
had been shot in the chest.

He pointed and Rachel saw the dead man.
She reacted with a quick intake of breath and
a low-volume sigh.

The door to the office was ajar. They
moved toward it and Bosch pushed it open
while Walling covered them from behind.
Bosch stepped in and saw Alicia Kent sitting
on the floor, her back to the wall.

He crouched beside her. Her eyes were
open but dead. A gun was on the floor between her feet and the wall behind her was
spattered with blood and brain matter.

Bosch turned and surveyed the room. He
understood the play. It was set up so it would
look like Alicia Kent had grabbed the agent's

gun from his holster, shot him and then sat down on the floor and took her own life. No note or explanation, but it was the best Maxwell could come up with in the short amount of time and opportunity that he had.

Bosch turned to Walling. She had let her guard down and was just standing there looking at the dead agent.

"Rachel," he said. "He's gotta still be here."

He stood and moved toward the door so he could search the squad room. As he glanced through the window he saw movement behind the electronics racks. He stopped, raised his weapon and tracked someone moving behind one of the racks toward a door with an exit sign on it.

In a moment he saw Maxwell break free of the cover and dash toward the door.

"Maxwell!" Bosch yelled. "Stop!"

Maxwell spun and raised a weapon. At the same moment that his back hit the exit door he started firing. The window shattered and glass sprayed across Bosch. He returned fire and put six shots into the opening of the exit door but Maxwell was gone.

"Rachel?" he called without taking his eyes off the door. "Okay?"

"I'm fine."

Her voice came from below him. He knew she had hit the floor when the shooting had started.

"Which exit is that door?"

Rachel stood up. Bosch moved toward the door, glancing at her, and saw glass all over her clothes and that she had been cut on the cheek.

"Those stairs go down to his car."

Bosch ran from the room toward the exit door. He opened his phone as he went and pushed the speed dial for his partner. The call was answered on half a ring. Bosch was already in the stairwell.

"He's coming down!"

Bosch dropped the phone and started down the stairs. He could hear Maxwell running on the steel steps below and instinctively knew that he was too far ahead.

TWENTY-TWO

BOSCH COVERED THREE MORE LANDINGS, taking three steps at a time. He could now hear Walling coming down behind him. He then heard the booming sound from below as Maxwell hit the exit door at the bottom. There were immediate shouts and then there were shots. They came so close together it was impossible to determine which had come first or how many shots had been fired.

Ten seconds later Bosch hit the exit door. He came out onto the sidewalk and saw Ferras leaning against the back bumper of Maxwell's fed car. He was holding his weapon with one hand and his elbow with the other.

A red rose of blood was blooming on his shoulder. Traffic had stopped in both directions on Third and pedestrians were running down the sidewalks to safety.

"I hit him twice," Ferras yelled. "He went that way."

He nodded in the direction of the Third Street tunnel under Bunker Hill. Bosch stepped closer to his partner and saw the wound in the ball of his shoulder. It didn't look too bad.

"Did you call for backup?" Bosch asked.

"On the way."

Ferras grimaced as he adjusted his hold on his injured arm.

"You did real good, Iggy. Hang in there while I go get this guy."

Ferras nodded. Bosch turned and saw Rachel come through the door, a smear of blood on her face.

"This way," he said. "He's hit."

They started down Third in a spread formation. After a few steps Bosch picked up the trail. Maxwell was obviously hurt badly and was losing a lot of blood. It would make him easy to track.

But when they got to the corner of Third and Hill they lost the trail. There was no blood on the pavement. Bosch looked into the long Third Street tunnel and saw no one moving in the traffic on foot. He looked up and down Hill Street and saw nothing until his attention was drawn to a commotion of people running out of the Grand Central Market.

"This way," he said.

They moved quickly toward the huge market. Bosch picked up the blood trail again just outside and started in. The market was a two-story-high conglomeration of food booths and retail and produce concessions. There was a strong smell of grease and coffee in the air that had to infect every floor of the building above the market. The place was crowded and noisy and that made it difficult for Bosch to follow the blood and track Maxwell.

Then suddenly there were shouts from directly ahead and two quick shots were fired into the air. It caused an immediate human stampede. Dozens of screaming shoppers and workers flooded into the aisle where Bosch and Walling stood and started running toward them. Bosch realized they were going to be run over and trampled. In one motion he moved to his right, grabbed Walling around the waist and pulled her behind one of the wide concrete support pillars.

The crowd moved by, and then Bosch looked around the pillar. The market was now empty. There was no sign of Maxwell but then Bosch picked up movement in one of the cold cases that fronted a butcher shop at the end of the aisle. He looked again closely and realized that the movement came from behind the case. Looking through the front and back glass panels and over the display of cuts of beef and pork, Bosch could see Maxwell's face. He was on the ground, leaning his back against a refrigerator in the rear of the butcher shop.

"He's up ahead in the butcher shop," he whispered to Walling. "You go to the right and down that aisle. You'll be able to come up on his right."

"What about you?"

"I'll go straight on and get his attention."

"Or we could wait for backup."

"I'm not waiting."

"I didn't think so."

"Ready?"

"No, switch. I go head-on and get his attention and you come around the side."

Bosch knew it was the better plan because she knew Maxwell and Maxwell knew her. But it also meant she would face the most danger.

"You sure?" he asked.

"Yes. It's right."

Bosch looked around the pillar one more time and saw that Maxwell had not moved. His face looked red and sweaty. Bosch looked back at Walling.

"He's still there."

"Good. Let's do it."

They separated and started moving. Bosch quickly moved down an aisle of concessions one over from the aisle that ended at the butcher shop. When he came to the end he was at a Mexican coffee shop with high walls. He was able to protect himself and look around the corner at the butcher shop. This gave him a side view behind the counter. He saw Maxwell twenty feet away. He was slouched against the refrigerator door, still holding his weapon in two hands. His shirt was completely soaked in blood.

Bosch leaned back into cover, gathered himself and got ready to step out and approach Maxwell. But then he heard Walling's voice.

"Cliff? It's me, Rachel. Let me get you some help."

Bosch looked around the corner. Walling was standing out in the open five feet in front of the deli counter, her gun down at her side.

"There is no help," Maxwell said. "It's too late for me."

Bosch recognized that if Maxwell wanted to take a shot at her the bullet would have to go through both the front and back glass panels of the deli case. With the front plate set at an angle it would take a miracle bullet to get to her. But miracles did happen. Bosch raised his weapon, braced it against the wall and was ready to shoot if he needed to.

"Come on, Cliff," Walling said. "Give it up. Don't end it like this."

"No other way."

Maxwell's body was suddenly racked by a deep, wet coughing. Blood came to his lips.

"Jesus, that guy really got me," he said before coughing again.

"Cliff?" Walling pleaded. "Let me come in there. I want to help."

"No, you come in and I'm going to—"

His words were lost when he opened fire on the deli case, sweeping his gun and shooting out the glass doors all the way down. Rachel ducked and Bosch stepped out and straightened his arms in a two-handed grip. He held himself from shooting but keyed on the barrel of Maxwell's weapon. If the muzzle zeroed in on Walling he was going to shoot Maxwell in the head.

Maxwell lowered his weapon to his lap and started to laugh, blood rolling down from both corners of his mouth and creating a freak clown look.

"I think . . . I think I just killed a porter-house."

He laughed again but it made him start to cough once more and that looked painful. When it subsided he spoke.

"I just want to say . . . that it was her. She wanted him dead. I just . . . I just wanted her. That's all. But she wouldn't have it any other way . . . and I did what she wanted. For that . . . I am damned . . ."

Bosch took a step closer. He didn't think that Maxwell had noticed him yet. He took one more step and then Maxwell spoke again.

"I'm sorry," he said. "Rachel? Tell them I'm sorry."

"Cliff," Walling said. "You can tell them that yourself."

As Bosch watched, Maxwell brought his gun up and put the muzzle under his chin. Without hesitation he pulled the trigger. The impact snapped his head back and sent a spatter of blood up the refrigerator door. The gun dropped onto the concrete floor between his outstretched legs. In his suicide Maxwell had adopted the same position as his lover, the woman he had just killed.

Walling came around the case and stood next to Bosch and together they looked down at the dead agent. She said nothing. Bosch checked his watch. It was almost one. He had ridden the case from beginning to end in little more than twelve hours. The tally was five dead, one wounded and one dying of radiation exposure.

And then there was himself. Bosch wondered if he was going to be part of the tally by the time all was said and done. His throat was now blazing and there was a feeling of heaviness in his chest.

He looked at Rachel and saw blood running down her cheek again. She would need stitches to close the wound.

"You know what?" he said. "I'll take you to the hospital if you take me."

She looked at him and smiled sort of sadly.

"Throw in Iggy and you've got yourself a deal."

Bosch left her there with Maxwell and walked back to the Million Dollar Theater building to check on his partner. While he was on his way, backup units were pulling in everywhere and crowds were forming. Bosch decided he would leave it to the patrol officers to take charge of the crime scenes.

Ferras was sitting in the open door of his car, waiting for the paramedics. He was holding his arm at an awkward angle and was clearly in pain. The blood had spread on his shirt.

"You want some water?" Bosch asked. "I've got a bottle in my trunk."

"No, I'll just wait. I wish they'd get here."

The signature siren of a fire-rescue paramedic truck could be heard in the distance, getting closer.

"What happened, Harry?"

Bosch leaned against the side of the car and told him that Maxwell had just killed himself as they had closed in on him.

"Hell of a way to go, I guess," Ferras said. "Cornered like that."

Bosch nodded but kept silent. As they waited his thoughts carried him down the streets and up the hills to the overlook, where the last thing Stanley Kent ever saw was the city spread before him in beautiful shimmering lights. Maybe to Stanley it looked like heaven was waiting for him at the end.

But Bosch thought that it didn't really matter if you died cornered in a butcher shop or on an overlook glimpsing the lights of heaven. You were gone and the finale wasn't the part that mattered. We are all circling the drain, he thought. Some are closer to the black hole than others. Some will see it coming and some will have no clue when the undertow of the whirlpool grabs them and pulls them down into darkness forever.

The important thing is to fight it, Bosch told himself. Always keep kicking. Always keep fighting the undertow.

The rescue unit turned the corner at Broadway, working its way around several stopped cars before finally braking at the mouth of the alley and killing the siren. Bosch helped his partner up and out of the car and they walked to the paramedics.

ACKNOWLEDGMENTS

This is a work of fiction. In making it up the author relied upon the help of several experts in the fields the story moved across. Most notably the author wishes to thank Drs. Larry Gandle and Ignacio Ferras for patiently responding to every question put to them in regard to the practice of oncology, medical physics and the use and handling of cesium. In the field of law enforcement, the author would be lost in the woods without the help of Rick Jackson, David Lambkin, Tim Marcia, Greg Stout and a few others who prefer anonymity. Any mistakes or exaggerations in these areas contained in *The Overlook* are purely the fault of the author.

The author also wishes to acknowledge the editorial help and generosity of Asya Muchnick, Michael Pietsch, Bill Massey and Jane Wood as well as Terrill Lee Lankford, Pamela Marshall, Carolyn Chriss, Shannon Byrne, Jane Davis and Linda Connelly.

ABOUT THE AUTHOR

Michael Connelly originally created *The Overlook* as a sixteen-part serial for the *New York Times Magazine.* However, he has expanded it substantially for this first hardcover edition. Connelly is a former journalist and author of the bestselling series of Harry Bosch novels, along with the bestselling novels *The Lincoln Lawyer, Chasing the Dime, Void Moon, Blood Work,* and *The Poet.* He has won numerous awards for his journalism and novels, including an Edgar Award.